Indigo and the Strange Animal Menagerie

C J Gloucester

A CIP catalogue record of this book is available from the British Library

ISBN: 978-0-9556534-1-4

To my very own Indigo.

'Brilliantly written with tremendous imagination, C J Gloucester manages to capture the feelings and emotions of a sensitive young girl which will instantly appeal to any child or adult who has an interest in the alternative. With detailed descriptions on meditation and raising issues concerning animal trafficking and the slums of Brazil, Indigo will inspire and enchant all who read it.'

Lucy Jenkins, Cotswold Life

'An imaginative, well-written story, moving between Gloucestershire and Brazil, with thought-provoking themes concerning animal welfare and the difficulties of being "different". A good read. Recommended.'

Jill Evans, Author of Gloucester Book of Days

'The story bowls along nicely with a lively pace and interesting relationships between well-drawn characters. It was good to see positive relationships between single parents and their children, and not the automatic assumption that singledom = misery and poverty for all involved. How refreshing! The ending sets the reader up to expect a sequel, which is good, as young readers hunger for series!'

Debbie Young, ALLi

PROLOGUE

Indigo was feeling strange.

She had felt like that for most of her life. Even as a small child, she had the sense of being different, special in some way; that there was something about her that placed her on the outside. Strange things had been happening to her recently. Things she couldn't tell anyone about. They began just a few days after her twelfth birthday. Vivid dreams, in vibrant colours; more like real experiences than dreams so that when she woke up she was left with the odd feeling of not knowing whether it had been a dream or whether it had actually happened.

Then there were the 'knowings' as she called them. She would 'know' something before it happened.

Then there was the school trip…

CHAPTER ONE

Indigo was really looking forward to a break from the dreary timetable of lessons. Mr Bell, her music teacher, had organised a trip to Colston Hall in Bristol for a music workshop. She had enjoyed the workshop but it had been a long day and everyone was now feeling tired and hungry.

They were standing on the corner of a busy main road waiting for the school bus to pick them up. Kieran, a wiry boy, all ears and teeth like a plasticine model, was getting on Indigo's last nerve with his silly, unfunny jokes.

'What's a Mummy's favourite music?'

Before Kieran could deliver the punch line, Jonathan, who was supposed to be Kieran's best friend, delivered it for him.

'Yeah, we know it's 'rap', he groaned, adding, 'you told us that one at lunchtime.'

'Yawn, yawn,' said another, waving his hand in front of his open mouth.

Kieran pushed Jonathan who pushed him back and before long the whole class was pushing and shoving and bumping into innocent people passing by who were not part of the argument. Kieran stood on Indigo's foot so she gave him a sharp elbow in the side and pushed him away. Mr Bell intervened and told them to behave.

Indigo, walked away from the group.

Boys are so irritating at times.

Standing on the kerb, she rubbed her eyes with the flat of her palms hoping to rub the tiredness away. As she did so, a vision of a canary yellow bus flashed across her mind's eye.

It was then she felt the 'knowing'.

In that micro second her mood changed from mild irritation and dragging tiredness to full alertness and pumping adrenaline as she became aware of the imminent danger threatening her and her school friends.

What should she do? How could she explain what she had seen? Who would believe her and anyway if they did, would she just end up causing mass pre-teen hysteria in a busy city centre street?

There was no time to be analytical. Ahead of her she could see a pavement ice cream seller. A moment of divine inspiration filled her with hope.

'Free ice cream,' she shouted as loud as she could, pointing in the direction of the cart, 'he's giving out free ice cream!'

She grabbed the nearest hand to her which was Mathew's and dragged him down the street away from the corner and towards the ice cream cart. The combination of 'free' and 'ice cream' seemed to have had the desired effect. The entire class began running towards the cart. There was a desperate rush to get there first before the supply of free ice cream ran out.

Even Freddie joined in the race displaying remarkable lightness of limb. Indigo had never seen him move so fast. Behind her she could hear Mr Bell shouting at the children to stop. Thankfully, on this occasion, no-one was taking any notice. She swung round to see a yellow bus swerving from side to side towards the street corner at an alarming speed. At the wheel was a portly, red faced man, with a terrified expression, one hand on the steering wheel, the other clutching at his chest.

The bus mounted the pavement, slammed into the metal litter bin Indigo had been standing next to, moments before, and skidded into the window of the building they had all been standing in front of. Indigo watched as the bus disappeared through the plate glass window. The sound of cracking glass, smashing bricks and the choking smell of building dust and burning brake fluid anchored her to the pavement. The group of excited children fell silent. Freddie, who liked his food, a fact demonstrated by the folds of skin hanging over the belt of his trousers like squidgy meringues, was the first to speak.

'Where's the free ice cream?' he asked, looking around him as if he'd lost something.

Mr Bell turned to look at Indigo. With an exaggerated raised eyebrow and a quizzical look he answered.

'I'm not sure if there ever was any free ice cream, Freddie.'

The others also turned to look at her.

Were they all thinking the same thing?

She looked away, avoiding eye contact. From the silence emerged a stream of screaming, disorientated children from the back of the bus. Without thinking Indigo ran towards them. She couldn't get the image of the poor bus driver's face out of her mind. She needed to know if he was all right.

She picked her way through mangled seats and strewn lunch boxes to the front of the bus. The windscreen had shattered and the metal frame had crumpled like sweet papers in a child's hand. She could see the bus driver's head slumped forward onto his chest. She was vaguely aware of the muted sounds of an ambulance and a fire engine somewhere in the distance. The bus was eerily quiet. There was a strange smell as she approached the still figure of the driver.

A smell unlike anything she could describe or had smelt before and one she would never forget filled her senses. She leaned across to look at him. He was slumped at an angle, his bulky frame squashed behind the steering wheel. His ruddy face was contorted into an expression of pain and his eyes stared ahead of him, unseeing. He was dead.

A vibration coming from the floor beneath disturbed her. It was a paramedic carrying his first aid kit. He placed his hand on Indigo's shoulder and steered her towards a female paramedic behind him. Indigo felt like she was in a dream, a very calm dream as she was led out of the bus.

Once outside, the noise of traffic, the whirring of emergency alarms and the cries of children brought her back from her inner world. She heard Mr Bell's voice.

'You okay, Indigo?'

She looked up at him and in a daze she said, 'I'm fine Mr Bell. The bus driver's dead.'

'I should have stopped you from getting on that bus. What's your mother going to say when she finds out?'

'It's okay, Mr Bell. My mother will be fine about it.'

'Are you sure? I don't want any trouble.'

Indigo could see that Mr Bell was in shock. She put her hand on his arm.

'I'm okay, honestly. My mother will be pleased that I did what I could to help. Don't worry.'

She noticed the tension in his shoulders relax.

'Well, I suppose if you hadn't acted like you did when you did, it might have been much worse. Strange really,' he said, rubbing his beard, 'It was as if you knew what was going to happen before it did.'

For an instant Indigo thought her secret was out but it was only Mr Bell's confused thoughts.

'Incredible really,' he muttered, as he walked away.

Indigo said nothing. She was exhausted. Back on the school bus, which had finally arrived to take them home, her classmates clamoured around, shouting out questions, wanting to know the gory details about the bus driver.

What did a dead person look like? Was there lots of blood? They had obviously watched too many horror movies, she thought as she sat down, trying to avoid answering them. It somehow seemed disloyal to the bus driver and his dignity.

Taking out her iPhone she pushed the earphones into her ears, leaned back in the seat and turned her face away to look out of the window. Once they realised she wasn't going to indulge them in their macabre voyeurism, they gave up and sat in their seats, leaving Indigo alone with her thoughts.

How had she known that an accident was about to happen and that her friends were in danger? Why did that image flash into her mind? Had she had a brief glimpse into the future?

The image of the bus driver with his vacant, staring eyes kept replaying in her head like a DVD stuck on replay. Her head was a jangle of thoughts, images and loud music. The start of a headache formed between her eyes. She rubbed the bridge of her nose and closed her eyes.

Breathing in deeply to calm herself, she concentrated on the spot in the middle of her brow, the spot her mother called the 'third eye'. It never failed to work. Moments later, her heart and her mind had stopped racing. A relaxed feeling, soothing and comforting filled the very cells in her body. With an unquestioning certainty, she realised her life would never be the same again.

She couldn't wait to get home and tell her mother.

CHAPTER TWO

The next morning Indigo woke to the gentle and soothing sounds of cymbals tinkling. Opening her eyes and looking across at her clock she saw it was 7am. Smiling to herself, she turned over and pulled the warm covers close. The soothing sounds were coming from her mother's bedroom. Indigo snuggled down waiting for her mother to come into her room and persuade her to wake up.

The door opened and in glided her mum, Demelza, looking like she had just walked out of a Pre-Raphaelite painting. Her auburn hair glinted like burnished copper as she drifted past arrows of early morning sunshine streaking across the room.

'Morning darling. Time to get ready for school.'

'Just two more minutes' she pleaded, pulling the warm duvet tighter around her.

Mornings weren't her favourite time of day. She would always try to get a few extra precious minutes in bed. Snoozing and daydreaming was how she liked to spend most of her time and it was especially pleasant underneath a cosy duvet, half asleep.

'Two more minutes, then up and get ready. Okay?'

'Okay,' she replied, burying herself deeper into the duvet.

Half an hour later, Indigo dragged herself out of bed, pulled on her school uniform and walked downstairs. She wandered into the kitchen, half asleep. Demelza took one look at the uncombed mess of flaxen hair, straggling over her shoulders and sent her back upstairs to finish getting ready.

When she finally re-appeared, her hair neatly brushed back in a ponytail, her pale skin pinking from the fresh scrubbing it had just received, she sat at the breakfast bar and helped herself to cereal.

'You look tired, Indigo. Did you sleep all right?'

'I do feel a bit tired,' she replied, concentrating on drizzling honey from a stainless steel twizzle stick.

'Well, it's not surprising after what happened yesterday. Do you want to talk about it?'

'Not really. I'd rather tell you about this strange dream I had last night,' she said, as she continued to drizzle.

'Don't you think you've had enough of that? I know you like making the patterns but have you considered your teeth?'

'Oops,' said Indigo snapping the top back on.

Demelza watched as Indigo chewed her food and gazed out of the window. She was in one of her daydreams.

'Come back into my world,' Demelza said, waving her hands at Indigo, 'Are you still in the dream?'

'Kind of. I can't seem to shrug off the feelings I had when I was in the dream.'

'It's just your mind trying to make sense of yesterday's events, I imagine.'

'It wasn't a bad dream, you know, not like a nightmare or anything and totally unconnected to what happened yesterday. Just really weird.'

Demelza took her coffee from the kitchen bench and sat at the breakfast bar with her. 'This sounds interesting.'

'I was in this dark forest, like a tropical rainforest you see on those nature programmes and I was running through the trees. I seemed to be running towards something not away from it. It seemed like I was running for ages. I started to feel exhausted.'

'No wonder you're so tired,' Demelza said.

Indigo continued. 'I tripped over a tree root and when I looked up I saw a small boy standing over me. He looked like one of those boys you see in the National Geographic from undiscovered tribes. He was staring at me and behind him there seemed to be a group of older men carrying cages – only I couldn't see what was in the cages. It was like a frozen scene. I was looking at them and they were looking at me. Then the boy moved towards me and I got the feeling he was going to say something.'

'What did he say?'

'I don't know. I woke up then.'

'Mmmn,' Demelza replied as if she were thinking long and hard on a problem.

'What do you think it means, mum?'

Indigo liked to ask her mother about the meaning of dreams.   Dreams were nearly always related to something happening in your everyday life.   But what would a tropical rainforest have to do with her life? She couldn't make sense of that.

'Perhaps it's portentous?' her mother replied, raising one eyebrow with a hint of a smile upon her lips.

'What's 'portentous' mean?' Indigo asked through a mouthful of cereal.

'It means predicting something that might happen to you. Something significant.'

'You mean I might be travelling to somewhere exotic?'

Indigo looked up at her mother with an expression of excitement.

'Who knows? You'll have to see what the universe has in store for you.'

Demelza left the breakfast bar and busied herself at the kitchen sink.

'Come on,' she urged, changing the subject, 'you'll be late for school.'

She was feeling too tired to pursue the topic further. She carried on eating her breakfast in silence, daydreaming about far away adventures. After a few mouthfuls, she looked up at her mother who was still at the kitchen sink.

'I'd miss you, mum, if I went far away.'

Demelza spun round and smiled. 'I'd miss you too.'

Indigo finished her breakfast, gathered up her books and giving her mum a hug, left for school. She walked to school every morning regardless of the weather. She enjoyed this part of her day when she could be alone with her thoughts and enjoy the changing seasons. The first show of snowdrops in the winter; the blaze of yellow daffodils in the spring and perfumed roses when summer finally arrived.

Part of her walk to school took her across the village. She disliked this bit of the walk. The noise of the rush hour traffic and the smell of the diesel fumes intruded upon her internal dialogue but it was only a small part of the way and she was soon across and going down the quiet lane that led to school.

When she arrived at school, she loaded her coat and books into her locker and made her way to the classroom. Ahead of her, in the corridor stood Georgina and her fellow tormentors. Indigo sighed. Georgina was in the year above Indigo and never missed an opportunity to harass her. Indigo knew what to expect. She was ready for them.

Time to use the 'negative energy shielding' technique her mother had taught her. As she walked towards the group, she focused on her breathing and imagined a pure, white light, like a stream of energy shooting through her into her heart.

Wham.

Her heart was now full to bursting with pure energy, which she now directed at Georgina.

Wham.

As Indigo tried to pass, Georgina blocked her way, standing tall and menacing, her cronies crowding in close to watch and learn.

'On your own again,' Georgina said looking down at her, 'no mates today?'

'Who'd want to be mates with her?' whined Sophie, Georgina's best friend and protégé.

'No one wants to be your friend and join you at the bottom of the food chain, do they?' Sophie taunted.

'Had any more visions, freak?' another taunted.

Georgina thrust her face into Indigo's so that she was inches away from her. Indigo recoiled. She hated it when anyone invaded her personal space but undaunted and feeling protected she fixed her stare back at Georgina. They stood like this for a few seconds although it seemed much longer than that to Indigo. She could feel Georgina's aggression like a pulse.

The trick with bullies, her mother told her, was never to let them see you have a weakness or that you're scared of them – even if you are. Georgina must have felt something as she straightened up, flicked her hair and walked away. As she did so, she called back at her, 'loser'. Georgina's cronies, like slaves to a master, followed her, each one taking their turn at pushing into Indigo, their laughter and jeering echoing along the corridor.

'Peace be with you,' Indigo chanted under her breath, as she carried on unfazed to her classroom.

She had learned from her mother that if people were being negative towards her she should deflect that negativity with a positive flow of energy and inner peace. Eventually, her mother had assured her, those people would stop being horrible. It wasn't working with Georgina.

Obviously, it took a lot longer with some people.

CHAPTER THREE

As she neared the classroom, she remembered that the new boy was starting school today and she wondered what he was like. When she opened the door and saw him sitting at her table, the strangest of feelings overcame her. She had a strong sensation of 'déjà vu', the feeling you get when you think you've experienced something before, as if you've lived that very same moment, maybe in a past life. The feeling lingered only for a few moments. She tried to stay with it to see if she could remember more but it was gone.

There was the usual hustle and bustle in the classroom as she walked over to her desk. Indigo sat with five other children. The two girls, Courtney and Shannon talked all the time and passed messages to each other on bits of paper. This was a problem for Indigo as she could be so easily distracted, especially if it was a subject she wasn't interested in. The others were three boys. Tom, the ginger haired, football mad lout. George, the classroom fool who was always larking about and Mathew who was preferred Mathew although George did make her laugh a lot and she liked that.

Today, however, the new boy was sitting where Mathew usually sat. His hair was dark and spiky and his skin well-tanned. He looked Mediterranean or perhaps Middle Eastern.

Quite handsome, but why move Mathew? Why not nerdy, annoying Tom?

Despite her disappointment, she smiled at him. He smiled back at her, his brown eyes shining. For the second time that morning she had a feeling of 'déjà vu'. Only this time it lingered a little longer. She had the strangest feeling that she'd known this boy before.

But how could that be? She'd never seen him before. Perhaps in a previous life?

She was jolted out of her thoughts by the teacher, Mr Lewis.

'Are you joining us today, Indigo? If so, please take your seat.'

'Sorry, sir,' she muttered, sliding into her seat next to Shannon.

She hadn't realised she'd been standing there for such a long time.

Mr Lewis was Welsh, quite rotund in shape with an untidy beard. He loved rugby and had a sing-song voice which boomed around the classroom. The children were a little bit afraid of him and so when he said 'sit down and be quiet' they generally did so. He called the class to order.

'Good morning,' he boomed.

'Morning Mr Lewis,' the class chorused back.

'Before we start this morning I want to introduce you to our new class member...' Mr Lewis placed his hand on the new boy's shoulder. 'Brandon Berenger. Brandon is from America and so I hope you will show him how friendly we all are at this school and give him a warm welcome.'

America? Interesting.

She had never met anyone from America before. How cool was that. She looked across at him and he gave her that smile again. All through the lesson, whilst Courtney and Shannon passed messages to each other on bits of paper, George fidgeted on his seat and Tom gazed dim-wittedly out of the window, Indigo was aware of the new boy sitting across from her. Occasionally, she glanced across at him to see if he was looking at her. Only once did she look up to be met by his chocolate-coloured eyes. He had a kind face, she decided. She thought about how she might feel being a new girl in school, joining part way through the term and decided to ask him if he wanted to join her for lunch. Besides, she felt she needed to find out more about this boy and whether she may have met him somewhere before.

The lesson continued until the bell rang. The class descended into noisy chaos with books slammed shut and then stuffed into rucksacks. Indigo approached Brandon who was packing his books, one at a time, into his rucksack.

'Hi. I'm Indigo. I'll show you where we have lunch if you like?'

'Sure, that'd be cool. What did you say your name was?'

'Indigo,' she repeated, her voice calm, enunciating the word 'Indigo' and waiting for his reaction.

She was used to people commenting on her name. Depending on which reaction she got she could mentally place them into two categories. Cool or weird. The cool type were often those with what she called an 'open mind', eager to learn new things and slow to judge people. The weird ones were those she referred to as 'closed off'. That's to say they weren't interested in new ideas and they usually didn't end up being her friend. Georgina and her cronies had been placed into the latter category.

'Cosmic name,' he replied, flashing his broad smile.

Indigo smiled back pleased he was in the cool group.

Lunch was in the school canteen where the children helped themselves from a selection of freshly cooked food. Brandon stared for a while at the choices on offer.

'No burgers?' he enquired in a mocking tone.

'We're lucky at this school,' explained Indigo, 'we have our own kitchen and cook serves up some scrummy meals. It's all part of this healthy eating thing, you know?'

It was obvious that he didn't know by the look on his face.

'Everyone's worried about us kids getting fat,' she added.

'Tell me about it!' he replied, 'we Americans invented fat kids!'

Indigo laughed as she piled her plate.

'So why aren't you fat?' she asked, still laughing.

'Must have skipped a gene,' he said, piling his plate with a mountain of food.

They sat at an empty table eating their food in silence. Brandon ate his meal as if it were his last, the food vanishing from his plate within minutes like a speeded up film. He sat back and pushed his tray away.

'Hey, that was good.'

'Is this your first time in England?' she asked, thinking perhaps he had been here before and that was where she'd met him.

'My very first time. So far I like it. You ever been to the States?'

'No,' she replied, her mind still pre-occupied with where she might know him from. 'I know this is going to sound strange but have we ever met before?'

'No, I don't think so. Why do you ask?'

'Oh, nothing.'

Indigo thought that if she wasn't careful he might morph from the cool to the weird group and she didn't want that to happen. She changed the subject. They sat in silence for a few moments then Brandon asked her where she got her unusual name from.

'My mother called me that the day I was born. She said I had an indigo-coloured aura.'

Again, she waited for his reaction.

'An indigo what?'

He sat up and leaned forward to hear her answer. She explained that an aura was a field of energy that surrounded the body.

'We all have them,' she continued, with some degree of authority since she was used to answering such questions, 'it's just that some people have a gift to see the energy colours and my mum has that gift.'

She spoke the last few words with pride.

'Your mum sounds cool.'

'She is,' Indigo agreed with him.

Oh wow! He is definitely in the cool group.

She remembered how her mother had explained to her how and why she'd chosen her name and about the fascinating world of auras and energy.

'Where did you get that from?' he pointed to the pendant she had round her neck.

'From my mum, she's an artist. She makes them. This was a special present, it represents my untapped potential.'

Brandon pulled a face, one she had seen many times before on other children's faces.

She knew what question was coming next and she was ready to answer it.

'Potential for what?'

'My psychic potential.'

Brandon looked even more puzzled than before.

'Psychic potential?'

She had struggled, at first, to explain what she meant by 'psychic potential' but she'd answered this question so many times before it just trotted off her tongue.

'Have you ever had the feeling when the phone rings, or someone knocks at your door, that you know who it is before you answer it?' she asked him.

He thought for a few moments and then a look of knowing fell across his face.

'Oh yeah. I know what you mean.'

'Well, that's you tuning into your psychic abilities only you probably haven't thought about it that way.'

He took a closer look at the pendant. It was made from platinum and coiled into three spiralling circles. Her mother had told her that the symbol represented her dormant feminine energy and her potential to be psychic. She remembered that conversation quite distinctly. Being a little unsure about the psychic thing and her mother telling her not to be concerned, that everyone was psychic to a degree. She remembered how powerful she had felt inside, how good it felt to be a girl.

Indigo was just beginning to feel relaxed talking to Brandon when she spotted Georgina coming towards them. Her stomach started to churn as she fretted about what Georgina would say or do in front of her new friend.

'Are you okay?' Brandon asked looking at Indigo's worried expression.

She was still watching Georgina, waiting to see if she was going to walk past and leave her alone for once. Georgina hesitated when she saw Brandon. To Indigo's relief, it seemed Georgina had decided to spare her from the usual verbal taunts. Instead, she slammed into Indigo's chair, on purpose, causing Indigo to knock over her drink.

'Oh I am so sorry. Silly me. Not looking where I was going.'

She was speaking in a silly little girl's voice Indigo had never heard her use before. It didn't match her size or personality.

Does she know how ridiculous she sounds?

Georgina smiled across at Brandon.

'Hey. No problem,' he said, apologizing on Indigo's behalf and smiling back.

'Oh, you're the new American boy everyone's been talking about. Hi, I'm Georgina. Do you want to come and sit with us over there?'

She pointed to where her cronies were sitting. The girls were staring at him.

'Err, maybe some other time?'

'Oh. Please yourself then.'

'Thanks. I will.'

'Oh, okay,' Georgina stammered.

She scowled at Indigo and walked back to her friends. Indigo went back to wiping the mess that was all over the table.

'Who's that?' Brandon asked when she'd gone, leaning back at a precarious angle.

'That's Georgina.'

'She seems a bit scary to me, a bit 'full on' as we say in the States.'

Indigo beamed at Brandon, 'I know what you mean. She can be a bit 'OTT' or 'over the top' as we say here in England,' mimicking Brandon's accent.

Despite all her good intentions, Indigo could feel hateful emotions brimming up within her towards Georgina.

'Peace be with you', she chanted to herself. 'Negative emotions are damaging to the soul'.

She was sure it would work on Georgina one day.

'I have to go now,' Indigo stood up, holding her tray, 'Maybe I'll see you around later?'

'How 'bout we meet up after school? You could show me the cool places to go in the village. That is if there is any?'

'I don't know about cool,' she laughed, 'but that'd be great. See you by the school gates at three?'

He smiled. 'Yeah, great.'

She left him sitting at the table. The feeling of 'déjà vu' had evaporated, replaced by a sense of joy at meeting a new friend.

CHAPTER FOUR

Indigo met Brandon by the school gates and they set off to walk towards the high street.

The village nestled in a valley in the heart of the Cotswolds and was made up of a main street, a few shops, two pubs and a community centre. In the centre of the village was one of Indigo's favourite places, the cemetery of the parish church. She loved to go there, sit under one of the yew trees and write in her secret journal.   It was so peaceful and if she stayed long enough and quiet enough the foxes that lived under one of the broken mausoleums would poke their noses out from under the tombstone and sniff around. Indigo would hold her breath so as not to make a sound and watch as they nosed their way out into the sunshine. At those special times, she felt very honoured to be so close to them.

The journal was a present from her mother. A Gratitude Journal. Her mum had given it to her for no other reason than she'd been feeling unhappy one day. Her mum told her to write down everything she was grateful for in her life and not to dwell on anything bad or negative. She said if she concentrated on all the positive things in her life and said thanks for them she would attract happiness. She'd been practising her mother's advice and found it was working.

The village of Painswick was split into three distinct areas. There was the posh area with huge, imposing houses, the not-so-posh area with some ordinary looking houses and the not-posh-at-all area which was the small council estate. Indigo showed Brandon the shortcut from the school to the high street, pointing out who lived where and any other little helpful information she thought he might be interested in. As they reached the main road, their conversation was drowned out by the noise of the lorries and cars rushing by.

They had been walking a few minutes when Indigo became aware of something ahead of them in the busy road. Brandon, oblivious to the events unfolding, continued talking fast in his loud American accent. Sensing something awful she stopped and grabbed hold of Brandon's arm to pull him back. They both froze, transfixed. It was like watching a DVD in 'still frame' mode. A feeling of helplessness came over them as they watched the scene play out in slow motion.

They saw the van, heard the excruciating screech of brakes being slammed and the smell of burning rubber. But worst of all was the sickening thud. Then the terrible screams and Indigo felt her stomach flip and the nausea rush over her. They ran towards the white van that had now come to a stop and where a small group of people had gathered round a distraught woman and her young child who was crying in the road. As they got closer they noticed a small bundle of ragged black fur. The bundle was a small dog, lying on its side, motionless. The driver had jumped out of his van and was arguing with a stout, little man.

'It wasn't my fault – it just ran out straight in front of me.'

'Don't give me that. You're all the same you white van drivers – always driving too fast. If you'd been watching your speed this wouldn't have happened,' the stout man shouted back at him.

Indigo looked on. The van driver continued to argue with the man. Onlookers jostled for position to see what all the fuss was all about, adding to the general chaos. The little girl knelt beside the dog, tears rolling down her pale cheeks. She was talking to the dog, coaxing the animal to show some sign of life.

'Come on, Bess, please wake up. Don't die,' she pleaded, the desperation showing in her voice.

The dog lay there motionless. Indigo moved closer. Brandon tried to stop her.

'It's okay,' she said, touching his arm.

She knelt down beside Bess. Her intense blue eyes seemed larger than ever as the daylight began to fade. The little girl looked up at Indigo, her eyes full of tears.

'Is she dead?'

'I'm not sure,' replied Indigo.

'Can you help her?'

The dog didn't appear to be breathing. There was no obvious sign of injury but that didn't mean much. Indigo had a limited knowledge of first aid and she knew there might be extensive internal bleeding from such a knock. She tucked her long hair behind her ears and, closing her eyes, laid her hands on the dog's lifeless form. Her hair fell over her face again but she was oblivious to it, concentrating all her energies on the dog.

The crowd grew silent as Brandon looked on in complete amazement. It was as if time was standing still. Even the van driver had stopped his squabbling and was staring at Indigo and the dog. It was imperceptible at first, perhaps the tiniest flick of her tail, the quivering of an eyelid, the twitch of an ear, then, yes, a weak whimper. Thick, black dog lashes flickered then the dog opened her large brown eyes. Seconds later, Bess was on her feet, wagging her tail.

'Oh Bess, Bess,' shrieked the little girl, 'you're all right.'

She was hugging Bess, crying and laughing all at the same time. The mother helped to wrap and swaddle Bess in her daughter's coat. Although still a little weak she managed several feeble licks of the little girl's face. The stunned crowd gasped in surprise. In the commotion Indigo slipped away unnoticed and found her way back to Brandon who was standing wide eyed and unblinking.

'Come on, let's go,' she urged and started back down the high street.

He caught up with her.

'What was that all about?' his voice a few octaves higher than normal.

Indigo replied, 'She wasn't ready to go.'

'What do you mean? 'Wasn't ready to go?'

'What happened back there?'

How could she explain what had really happened? She had just found someone she thought could be a good friend and she didn't want to lose him. He would think she wasn't quite right.

'I didn't do anything.'

'Come on now. I swear to God that dog was dead…Wasn't it?'

'I told you, she wasn't ready to go.'

'You did something back there. I know you did,' he persisted.

They were walking back towards Indigo's house now, Indigo setting the pace.

Should she tell him? What could she tell him? How could she explain? What would he think?

'I'd like us to be good friends, Brandon?'
'I don't see why we can't be?'
'I'm not sure if you'd understand?'
'Try me.'

CHAPTER FIVE

She stopped walking and turned to him. The light was beginning to fade, silhouetting an unusually large, harvest moon. It glowed a rich, golden colour, hanging low in the darkening sky like an oversized Christmas decoration. She looked him straight in the eyes. They were kind eyes. This was the moment. She decided to take a chance. For some reason she felt she could trust Brandon even though she hardly knew him. She sensed he would understand.

'I can do things…'

'Yeah …and?'

'What I mean is…I have a gift…'

'What do you mean - a gift?'

'Well, that's what my mum calls it. I can't quite explain.'

'Like you have special powers?'

'Sort of.'

She bit her lip, waiting for the inevitable.

'Cooool,' said Brandon, giving her a high five.

Oh, thank you Universe. Thank you for sending Brandon to me.

'Is that what happened yesterday with the bus?'

'Oh, you heard about that?'

'Everyone's talking about it at school,' he replied.

They had continued walking and were outside Indigo's house now.

'Here we are. This is where I live.'

She pointed to an impressive Cotswold stone house. The front garden had been landscaped and designed by someone with a flair for the unusual. Huge steel sculptures adorned the grounds reminding Brandon of the garden in the movie, Edward Scissorhands.

'Nice place.'

'I like it,' Indigo said. 'Want to come in?'

Brandon looked at his watch.

'Could do but I can't stay long. My dad will begin to wonder where I am.' They walked to the back of the house and in through the kitchen door. Demelza sat at a long and substantial French oak table which was cluttered with books. Some were wedged open, others had hand-made bookmarks protruding from the pages. The rich smell of coffee mixed with roast chicken filled the room. A dark grey cat sat on the table. They both looked up as Indigo and Brandon walked in. The cat stared at Brandon with a look that seemed to say, 'Who are you?'

'Hi mum. This is Brandon. He just started at my school today. Brandon this is my mum and this...' pointing to the cat, 'is Piewacket. He's mum's 'fam-il-i-ar',' she said, emphasizing each syllable.

Demelza raised her eyebrows in an exaggerated way and smiled. Brandon looked puzzled.

'It's okay Brandon. Just ignore her. She thinks I'm a witch and Piewacket's my,' she made speech marks, 'Familiar Spirit' aiding and abetting me with my spells. He's actually just a very lazy, very fat cat.'

She stroked his throat. Piewacket purred, did a 'roly-poly', messing up her papers, then stretched himself out, closed his gorgeous bronze eyes and went straight back to sleep.

'You don't mind if we go upstairs, do you?'

'Of course I don't mind. Just remember the rules.'

'Yes, mum. I know. As long as we clean up our mess.'

'That's all I ask.'

Demelza smiled at Brandon then carried on reading her books.

'Thanks mum. Come on Brandon, it's this way.'

They disappeared down the corridor and climbed the stairs. When they reached the landing, Indigo turned to Brandon and said, 'You'll have to excuse my mum, she's a bit of an old hippy.'

'Nothing wrong with hippies.' Brandon replied.

Pictures of animals and hand-made notices to *'KEEP OUT'* and *'BEWARE of the WILD ANIMALS'* covered Indigo's bedroom door.

'I guess you like animals?'

'I love animals. Don't you?'

'They're okay.'

Indigo put her hand on the door handle but didn't open the door.

'You need to take your shoes off before you go in.'

She saw his puzzled look.

'It's one of the rules.'

'Okay,' he shrugged, kicking off his trainers.

Indigo flung open the door and allowed Brandon to enter first.

'Wow!' exclaimed Brandon looking around him. 'This is amazing.'

He stepped onto the green shag pile carpet.

'This feels exactly like grass,' he said, as he stood in the middle of the room, admiring the decor and wiggling his toes through the carpet.

Indigo's room resembled a tropical rainforest. Tree creepers hung from a vaulted ceiling. In the centre of the room a palm tree stretched towards the apex and masses of thick foliage covered the walls. Hanging from wooden branches were a number of real-looking stuffed animals. A large black gorilla, a lemur hanging by its tail and on another branch hung a three-toed sloth. In one corner hiding in the undergrowth an Asian tiger crouched. A mosquito net hung above Indigo's bed completing the feeling of being at base camp in the deepest and darkest, undiscovered jungle of Borneo.

'This is a fantastic bedroom. I don't think I've ever seen anything quite like it. Your mum must be great to let you have all this in your bedroom.'

'My mum's brilliant.'

A noise from behind a closed door alerted Indigo's attention. Going towards the door, she continued.

'She likes to indulge me in my love for animals. You haven't seen the best yet,' she said, opening the door.

'You mean there's more?'

He noticed the smell first before he saw the cages, wall to wall, full of animals. This time they were real.

'This is Rosemary.'

She walked over to a glass tank built into the wall. 'She's a South American Rose Tarantula and she loves being picked up. Want to hold her?'

Brandon took several steps back. 'No thanks. I don't like spiders.' He shivered and rubbed his arms up and down as if he were feeling the cold.

'Okay. Let's move on.'

Indigo loved introducing her pets. She fell into the role of 'tour guide' like a professional. As she did the introductions, she checked that the animals had food and water and talked to them as if they were human. She was in her element.

'This is Bruce. He's a Common Garter snake.'

Brandon peered into the cage. A small black and yellow patterned snake seemed to be staring at him, its tongue flicking in and out.

'Don't worry,' Indigo re-assured him, 'it's not aggression. They use their tongue to detect odours. He's just sniffing you out.'

'And this is Gerry, my cute little Leopard Gecko.'

Brandon thought it looked like something out of an Australian Aboriginal painting.

'Mum doesn't like me keeping animals in cages. She says they should be allowed to live in their natural habitats, but I've managed to convince her that I'm helping with conservation.'

'Are you?' Brandon asked, not entirely convinced.'

I think I am but I'm not sure mum believes me. I think she just got sick of me going on about having a pet.'

'She's right really.'

'I know, but these are all captive bred,' Indigo added by way of justification.

From the look on Brandon's face she could see he wasn't convinced by that argument either.

CHAPTER SIX

Somewhere, in the back streets of Rio de Janeiro, a thin, grubby boy cowered in the corner of a very different animal menagerie.

He listened to the orders being barked out by Carlos at two men who were sitting at a table, smoking thin cigarettes and drinking glasses of Aguardente. They also listened, afraid to answer back or ask questions. No one questioned Carlos. Powerful and dangerous, he was not a man to be crossed. Carlos was pacing the room, shouting and kicking anything in his way. Then he smashed his fist on the table with such ferocity that the glasses jolted, causing their contents to spill. The men jumped up to avoid the spillage. Still they did not answer back.

'Do you understand me now?'

It wasn't really a question. Juan, the smaller of the two, spoke.

'Yes, Boss. We understand.'

He looked up at Carlos then looked away. When Carlos got this angry it was best not to look at him in case he took that as a challenge to his authority. Juan ran his fingers over the scar on his left cheek remembering the last time he had angered Carlos.

The animals, crammed into dirty cages, were distressed by Carlos's shouting and were squawking and screeching and thrashing about in their tiny cages.

'And you better shut these up. The whole favela can hear them.'

Chico, who was still cowering in the corner, listened to the tirade, not once looking up. To Chico, Carlos's eyes were like those of a shark, dead looking and utterly evil. As soon as Carlos walked into the room, Chico felt the atmosphere change from tranquil, when he was with his beloved animals, to menacing when he was around. Saying no more, Carlos strode out of the room, slamming the door behind him. The two men stared at each other, felt for their guns and turned to the small boy.

'You heard him. Shut this lot up. We have to go somewhere now. Just make sure you are here when we get back.'

They finished the remains of their drink and stood up. Domingo towered above the smaller man, Juan. His large hands swung by his sides as he walked, reminding Chico of an ungainly, giant gorilla. What Juan lacked in stature he made up for in meanness. Thin faced, with a hooked nose, Juan reminded Chico of a weasel. Chico always compared humans to animals. It was as though once he had categorised them, then he knew what he was dealing with. He understood animals much more than he understood humans. He liked animals more than humans too. At least when they were mean it was for a good reason, like when they were hungry. The two men left, slamming the door again.

Once they were gone Chico crept out from his corner. The animals were, by now, deeply distressed. Moving from cage to cage, he whispered comforting words to them. The animals appeared to know what he was saying, as if some secret code was being passed from one to the other. One by one they stopped their noise and became calm. When he had finished the room was quiet and peaceful. Chico walked over to the table and finished off the remains of a meal the men had left behind. He couldn't remember the last time he had eaten but his stomach felt empty. He drained the last dregs of what remained in their glasses, checked on the animals once more and then went to lie back on the mattress.

He pulled a few dirty rags around him and then rummaged around underneath the mattress for something, pulling out a torn and well fingered photo. It was of a pretty, young woman with long black hair. She was smiling at him.

He closed his eyes and dreamed of his mother. He dreamed that they were running on Ipanema beach, holding hands. They were both laughing; the wind was blowing his mother's long, black hair across her face. She stopped to kiss him, her body felt warm and smelled of candy. He lay there in the dark and fetid room, smiling and dreaming of his beautiful and treasured mother.

42

CHAPTER SEVEN

Back in Indigo's bedroom, Brandon continued to be impressed. He kept looking around the room and now and then he would discover another smaller animal amongst the creepers.

'I just can't get over the set up you have here. It's awesome.' He rolled his eyes as he said it and Indigo laughed.

'I buy all these animals from the World Wildlife Fund. I know then that I'm definitely contributing to animal conservation.'

Indigo sat down on her bed. She had hoped Brandon had forgotten about earlier. He sat down on her computer chair and swivelled it round to face her.

'So what was that all about earlier?'

Indigo considered ignoring him in the hope that he would forget all about it but she knew that wouldn't work.

She listened to her inner voice.

You can trust him. He will not betray your trust. Be brave.

'If I tell you, will you make me a solemn promise?'

'Promise,' he said, without hesitation, crossing his heart as he did so.

'Promise that you won't make fun of me and that you won't tell another living soul. I would be really hurt if you let me down.'

43

'We're buddies aren't we?'

'I guess so.'

I don't let buddies down.' He grinned. 'We can pledge if you like?'

'What does that involve?'

'It used to involve drawing blood...'

Indigo winced.

'It's okay,' he re-assured her, 'we don't have to do that now. Now you just make a verbal pledge. We decide what we want to pledge to each other – in this case – that I won't let you down and I won't tell any of this to another living soul. Then we compose a pledge and recite it together.'

'Sounds good. Okay. Do we begin 'I solemnly swear?'

'No. That sounds like you're about to give evidence in court. How about 'With this pledge?'

'That sounds like you're reciting marriage vows.'

They giggled, more out of embarrassment than anything else.

'Okay, okay. I've got it. This solemn pledge made between Indigo and Brandon will create a bond of friendship that will unite us forever. We pledge to never let each other down and anything we say to each other we agree is confidential stays confidential. We further pledge to never tell another living soul.'

'That's good but we need to say what happens if we break the pledge.'

'Yeah. Good idea.'

'If we break this pledge then we break the special friendship bond that exists between us.'

'It needs to be written down.'

Brandon reached for a pen from the desk and wrote it down. Indigo went into the other room and brought back a single candle on an ornate wrought iron stand.

'Candles are good for making affirmations. I think we should light one.'

'Cool by me.'

Indigo sat down cross-legged on the floor. She placed the candle in front of her and lit it. The flame cast flickering shadows across the jungle walls, creating a magical atmosphere. Brandon sat opposite and handed her the piece of paper.

And so there it was, in the candle lit room, amid the tropical jungles of Borneo, with silent but watchful animals gazing down upon them, a long and trusted friendship began.

CHAPTER EIGHT

Far away in a tropical rainforest, a small brown boy crouched in the dense undergrowth, watching his father's every move. His dark eyes darted from man to man, watching their every move and waiting for a signal. He didn't want to mess this up. His father had shown him great trust by allowing him on this trip.

'Papa, what happens now?' he whispered, his dark eyes wide and questioning.

'Silence, Itamar,' replied his father, through clenched teeth.

Itamar dropped his gaze to the ground, feeling the other men's scowling eyes on him. He realised his mistake and worried that his father would not let him come with him again. He had been looking forward to his first hunting expedition. In his village, it was a great honour for a young man to join the elders. It was part of the ritual of becoming a man. He wished he hadn't opened his mouth. He looked back at his father who was signalling, to the others to get into their positions. Itamar's muscles tensed. He was ready.

Having sensed danger, the forest animals grew quiet in the darkness beneath the forest canopy. Another signal was given by the elder, a wiry old man, and the group began their well-practised moves. The forest was no longer quiet. A united cacophony of terrified shrieks resounded beneath the canopy. Loud screeching, crashing of branches, rustling of foliage and men shouting as a large woven net came crashing through the undergrowth from above them, descending upon their prey.

Itamar sprang into action, concentrating on his newly learnt skills. The captured animals were writhing, jumping and screeching under the net. Itamar approached them, his steps tentative, talking in his native language. The animals turned to him, tilted their heads to one side and looked at Itamar with human-like eyes. He was close to them now. They had huddled together and had stopped screeching but appeared curious. He glanced across at his father who nodded his approval. Itamar wiped his brow and took a deep breath, nodding back to his father. He had passed the first test. It was over.

The forest fell silent again.

CHAPTER NINE

After the pledge-making Indigo knew she could tell Brandon everything so she told him all about her special gifts.

'I get feelings. I can't really explain. Have you ever heard of Indigo Children?'

'No. Never.'

'Mum told me, a long time ago, that I was an Indigo child and that as I got older I would develop special gifts. Well, recently they've started to emerge without me having to do anything. It's like I'm acting on pure instinct. It's as though I can communicate with animals but not through words. It's more of a feeling.'

'But the dog was dead, wasn't it? How could you communicate with a dead dog?'

'Like I said the dog wasn't ready to go. I could sense that she hadn't left her earthly body. She was in limbo – you know that place between life and death. I just guided her back towards her physical body. I just laid my hands on the dog and that's when I felt it. Like a powerful energy flowing through me. That's the only way I can describe it. You don't think I'm mad do you?'

'Not especially,' he replied, giving her an uncertain look. 'But I'm still not sure what did happen. Are you telling me you can bring animals back from the dead?'

'I suppose I am,' she told him.

Indigo cringed. 'Kind of. You're not spooked are you? You don't think I'm mad?'

'It is a bit spooky,' his voice became ghoulish; 'it's not every day I meet a girl who can bring back the dead.'

She shot him a look and threw a cushion at him. He feigned injury and lay there motionless for a few seconds as though dead.

'Just kidding. I thought you might be able to bring me back to life.'

'You said you wouldn't make fun of me.'

'I know and I won't but it's all a bit mind blowing. Give me a break and lighten up a little.'

'Sorry. It's just that you're the only one I've told about this. I wouldn't dare tell any of the other kids at school. They already think I'm some kind of weirdo. Georgina would make my life hell and that would be that. I'd end up getting bullied for the rest of my life.'

'Yeah. I've noticed some of those dudes can be pretty evil. Like the big tall girl – what's her name?'

'That's Georgina.'

'You wouldn't stand a chance against her - she'd flatten you.'

Indigo laughed. She had a vision of Georgina, pumped full of air like a large balloon, landing on her from a great height and being squished beneath her large frame.

Brandon's mobile phone interrupted them. A rap style American national anthem ring tone.

'Hi dad…Yeah, sorry, I should have rang sooner to let you know I was going to be late. Yeah, I'm fine. I'm round at a friend's house. I'll be home soon…Next ten minutes? Okay. Bye…I'd better go.   I didn't realise how late it was.'

'Sorry that's my fault. Should I ask my mum to give you a lift? It's pretty dark out there.'

'Okay. If you're sure she won't mind. I'm not sure if I know the way from here.'

'Mum's a star. She won't mind'

Indigo was right. Her mother hadn't minded at all. They turned into Brandon's drive where a dark blue Jaguar was parked in front of the garage. Demelza stopped the car, but left the engine running.

'Come on in. My dad likes to meet my friends.'

'It's getting late and we haven't eaten yet.'

Demelza, pulled on the hand brake.

'We really should get going,'

'It's not that late,' Indigo said.

They had lived in the village since Indigo could remember but her mother didn't socialise. Indigo thought it was because her mother was shy.

'Let's go in, mum,'

Indigo opened the car door. Brandon was already standing on the driveway, waiting. Demelza looked across at her daughter urging her to go inside and so relented. They walked to the side of the house and Brandon rang the bell. His father opened the door.

'And about time too. I was getting worried.'

'Dad, this is my friend, Indigo and her mum, Demelza. They offered to give me a ride home. This is my dad.'

Brandon's dad smiled, showing a row of straight, white teeth. 'Hi. I'm Luke. Come on in. Don't stand out there.'

They were ushered into a spacious open-plan living room with a huge roaring fire. Indigo made straight for the fire and stood there for a minute or two gazing into the flames before turning to look around the room.

'Can I get you a drink?' Luke asked Demelza, 'Coffee, tea, something stronger, a glass of wine?'

'Oh no, I'm driving. Coffee would be fine.'

He stood there staring at her for what seemed an age. Indigo could tell, by the way Brandon's dad was staring at Demelza, that there was some kind of attraction. She could literally 'feel the vibes'. It was obvious Brandon had sensed something too as he was looking from Demelza back to his dad and then across at Indigo. They smiled a quiet recognition at each other.

'Is it okay if we go up to my bedroom, dad?'

'Yeah that's fine by me,' he said, smiling at Demelza.

Demelza looked across at Indigo. 'Don't you think we should be going?'

Before Indigo could reply Luke interrupted.

'You've only just got here. I'll get that coffee on.'

Seeing their chance to escape upstairs, they disappeared from the room as if fleeing from an airborne virus, leaving Demelza alone with Luke.

CHAPTER TEN

Brandon's room was a typical American boy's bedroom. Large posters of American baseball players and rap artists Indigo had never heard of covered the walls. Indigo walked over to a very powerful telescope positioned by his window and looked through the lens.

'Are you a star gazer?'

'You could call it that. I'm seriously into astronomy. Ever since I saw my first supernova, I was hooked.'

'What's a supernova?' Indigo asked, looking through the telescope.

Brandon went over to his bookshelf and searched through his books. He brought out a large, hard back booked and flicked through it to a page which he opened out on his study desk for Indigo to see.

'Look, here's a picture of one.' The photo showed what looked like a huge brown egg split in two with a greenish inside and white light exploding from its insides.

'That looks like a picture of an aura.' Indigo said, flicking through the rest of the pages. 'But what is it exactly?'

'It's when a star dies and explodes.'

'Stars die?'

'Sure they do.' He flicked through the book to another page. 'Didn't you know the sun was the result of a supernova, four and a half billion years ago?' he added.

'No. I never knew that. I prefer astrology to astronomy,' Indigo said, her butterfly mind kicking in. 'I'm interested in how the stars affect our destinies. I find that much more fascinating. What sign are you? No wait, let me guess?'

Indigo studied Brandon, her arms crossed, index finger touching her chin, head slightly tipped to one side in a staged pose. Brandon could almost feel her looking right inside him, at his very soul. He shifted from one foot to the other.

'I think you're a Sagittarius. That means you're philosophic and adventurous. Am I right?'

Brandon thought for a moment before replying. 'Not even close. I'm a Leo. Does that mean I'm courageous like a lion?'

He made a roaring sound, clawing at the air.

'You're making fun of me again. You said you wouldn't do that…'

Brandon shrugged. 'How about you? What sign are you?'

'I'm an Aquarius. We're free thinkers, humanitarian and very unpredictable,' she replied, opening her arms wide and twirling around the room, like a Whirling Dervish, as if to emphasise her unpredictability.

Indigo's butterfly mind, once again, flipped onto an entirely unconnected subject.

'I think your dad fancies my mum.' She walked over to the bookshelf and scanned the books. 'Did you see the way he looked at her? I think he likes her. Did you feel the vibes? I've never known anyone attracted to my mum before. Most people in the village think she's weird. In fact I've never known her to have a boyfriend.' In a sudden attack of self-awareness, Indigo realised she was gabbling. 'Sorry. I sometimes get carried away. Just tell me to shut up.'

'Shut up,' he replied, a dead-pan look on his face, and then he laughed. 'I'm not sure if it was instant attraction but there was definitely something going on there.'

'Hey. Wait a minute. That's a bit out of order isn't it? What about your mum?' Indigo asked, realising Brandon's father would already have a wife.

'My Mom's dead.'

There was an embarrassed silence and then Indigo spoke.

'I'm sorry, I didn't realise...Well I just assumed...'

She was struggling to find the right words. She hadn't known anyone whose mum had died before. She couldn't imagine what that would be like to experience. She tried to think how she would feel if her own mother died. She shuddered.

Unthinkable.

'It's okay. Mom died two years ago. I'm cool about it now.'

'What happened?' Indigo asked, though she was not sure how she would react to the answer.

'She got cancer about five years ago. She had lots of treatment for it, and seemed to be getting over it but she had what dad said was 'a relapse' and she got really ill again, really quickly. Dad brought her home from the hospital and she died a couple of days later. I thought for a while that it was dad's fault because he took her out of hospital but we had a long talk one day and he told me that she knew she was going to die and she just wanted to be home when it happened.'

'Do you miss her?'

'I think about her every day. If I'm doing something I think to myself, 'Hey, Mom would have liked this'. I did miss her a lot at the beginning but I guess it's got easier in the last six months.'

'Mum says we don't die. She says our souls are eternal.'

Brandon changed the subject. 'What about your dad? You haven't said anything about him?'

'I don't know who my dad is. Mum's a single parent and she never talks about him. I don't know anything about him really. But I'm totally cool about that too. So I suppose it's okay for our parents to fancy each other?'

'I guess so.' Indigo placed the book she had been flicking through back on the bookshelf. She had a strange sense that her mother needed her.

'I think we should go back downstairs. I'm sure mum will want to be going home now. I'd better go.'

They made their way down stairs and into the lounge where her mother was sitting perched on the edge of an armchair looking out of place. Indigo could sense an awkward atmosphere as she entered the room.

'Hi mum. Do you want to go now?'

'Yes, I think we should.'

Demelza finished her coffee and stood up to leave.

'Must you go, so soon,' said Luke.

'Thank you but it's school tomorrow.'

Luke helped Demelza with her coat.

'I've been thinking of giving a party to get to know more people in the village,' he announced. 'I'd love it if you'd come?'

'She'd love to,' blurted Indigo, before her mother got the chance to refuse.

CHAPTER ELEVEN

Later that evening, Indigo looked up from the book she was reading and watched her mother glide towards her across her bedroom floor. Demelza never walked but always appeared to glide, thought Indigo, like the elegant and ethereal beings in her angel cards. Her mother sat down beside her on the bed. She often came into her bedroom at night for a chat or to ask how Indigo's day at school had gone.

'Mum,' Indigo began, 'something happened today that was really weird and I'm not sure what did happen but Brandon was there and I'm worried that he won't be my friend anymore and I don't know what to do about it and I'm worried he'll tell everyone at school.'

'It's not like you to be worried about such things?'

'I think it's because I really like him. I feel like he understands me even though I hardly know him and I don't want to lose his friendship.'

'If he's a true friend and he really does understand you then he's not going to be the type of boy who would jeopardise his friendship with you. If he does then he wasn't a good friend in the first place. Sadly, I'm afraid, we have to learn these lessons as we go along. It's all part of growing up.'

'I guess so. But it's so hard mum.'

'I know Darling but at the end of the day you only need to know who you really are and that is a beautiful girl in every way and no-one can take that away from you.' She moved a stray lock of hair and tucked it behind Indigo's ear. 'Anyway, what did happen today?'

Indigo told her about 'the dog incident' as she now referred to it.

'I didn't even think about what I was doing. It was as though I knew exactly what to do without being told. Like jumping into a river to save someone's life but not thinking about your own safety. Just instinct I guess. Brandon thinks I brought the dog back to life. Do you think I did?'

'I'm not sure. How did you feel when you put your hands on the dog?'

'Well. It felt like there was a powerful energy flowing from my body into the dog's body, then seconds later the dog seemed a lot better.'

'Do you know what I think,' she said, looking at Indigo with an understanding only mothers possess for their daughters, 'I think you are a very special child with many special gifts. Don't fight these feelings. Don't block the flow of energy. The universe holds many mysteries and sometimes we don't know how or why things happen. But in a way I don't think we need to know why, just that they do. There's so much we don't understand but we just have to be accepting and know that these things happen for good reasons. I think you have to be accepting of your special gifts. Listen to your inner voice; trust your instincts and 'go with the flow'.'

Indigo anticipated what she was going to say and joined in to end the old hippy phrase her mother often used. They made the peace sign and laughed. Demelza kissed Indigo and gave her a hug. Indigo squeezed her back.

'I love you mum.'

'I love you too. Now go to sleep.'

With that Demelza glided out of the room.

CHAPTER TWELVE

The next morning Indigo and her mother walked to school together as Demelza ran an art class every Tuesday morning. They both liked to comment on the school run in the village and found it quite amusing. It reflected the social hierarchy that existed. There were those mums who lived in the posh houses who drove their children to school in brand new, top of the range, four-wheel drives; those mums who aspired to living in the posh houses drove second hand, bottom of the range, four-wheel drives and those mums who lived on the council estate who walked to school.

Lauren's mum drove to school in a 'pimped-out' old sporty number. She would arrive at school late, brakes screeching, the loud thud, thud of rock music at the fragile hour of eight thirty in the morning with the window wide open, a cigarette, held between two yellowed fingers, hanging out of the car window. Indigo didn't know her but she secretly admired her for having the courage to be exactly who she wanted to be and not care a jot for what other people thought of her. She felt a little sorry for Lauren though because she sensed Lauren did care a lot about what people thought of her mother.

As they arrived at the school gates, she was aware of a slight buzz in the air as the mothers stood around in their little groups chattering. She was about to give her mother a kiss goodbye when a familiar voice said 'Good Morning'. She looked around. It was Luke. He was smiling at her mother. Indigo noticed the incessant chattering of the mothers ceased. All heads turned towards Luke and Demelza. They were like NASA satellites tuning in.

'Morning, Luke,' Demelza smiled back.

Indigo left her mother talking to Luke and began chatting to Brandon keeping an eye on what was happening close by. The gawping mothers were whispering. Indigo concentrated and listened in. That was another of her special gifts. She was able to tune into their frequencies, sometimes from quite long distances.

'Who's he?'

'He's rather dishy.'

'That's Brandon's father.'

'He's a single parent you know?'

'What's he doing talking to her?'

'Helloooooh,'

Indigo became aware of Brandon waving his hands in front of her face. 'Ah, you're back with us.'

'Sorry. Just day dreaming.'

She looked across at her mother who was smiling and nodding at Luke, then back at the mothers. They looked positively green with envy. Things were certainly going to change around here.

'Gotta go, mum.'

Demelza gave her a big hug and kissed her goodbye. Luke ran his hands through Brandon's thick spiky hair, mock punched him in the stomach and said, 'Go get'um kiddo.'

Strange American ritual.

Georgina and her cronies were on the school steps glaring at her as she went by. Indigo gave them the biggest smile she could muster. Although her mother had told her it was rude to 'listen in' to other people's conversations she couldn't resist on this occasion. It wasn't only her mother who was the cause of such jealousy this morning.

Over the next few weeks Indigo and Brandon became the best of friends, like kindred spirits. Indigo had always been considered a bit of an odd ball but since Brandon's arrival she had become a little more accepted. Demelza often reminded her, when she felt down, that she was 'a highly evolved being in a human body' and she had special gifts that would help humankind one day. Even as young as she was, Indigo knew her mother was right. She had always sensed she was different from the other girls at school, not better, just different. It set her apart from them. They often excluded her just because she was different. She was particularly hurt one day when Georgina approached her and Brandon in the school canteen. It was no secret that Georgina disliked Indigo. It was also no secret that she liked Brandon.

'Hi there, Brandon.'

She blanked Indigo by perching on the edge of the desk with her back to her.

'It's my birthday in two weeks and I'm having a party. I'd love you to come. Here's the invitation. You will come, won't you?'

'That depends.'

'Depends on what?' Georgina looked intrigued.

'Is there an invitation for Indigo?'

Georgina looked nonplussed for a moment.

She hadn't expected him to say that. Indigo could see she was facing a bit of a dilemma. Whether to show her true mean, spiteful self to Brandon and tell him that Indigo wasn't invited or to present Brandon with the pleasant, but utterly false, Georgina. She decided to play it safe.

'Of course Indigo is invited,'

She rummaged in her Cath Kidston school bag.

'That's strange. I don't seem to have her invitation with me. I must have left it at home.'

The lie was unconvincing.

'Oh, must go. I'm late. I'll bring it in tomorrow. Bye then.'

And with that she waltzed off to join her friends. Indigo sat with her head down, fingering some crumbs on the table.

'Don't worry. I wasn't taken in by that performance,' Brandon re-assured her.

Later that day, Brandon suggested they go into Gloucester after school to mooch around. Indigo thought it a great idea. She usually went straight home after school so she made a quick phone call to her mum to let her know she'd be late.

When they got on the bus to Gloucester they made straight for the back seat. It had been one of those crisp, sunny days when the warmth of the sun could still be felt and before the grey, cold skies of winter began. But by the time they got on the bus the sun had disappeared behind a slate-coloured cloud and it looked like rain.

'I hope it doesn't rain,' she said, looking out across the green expanse of the Painswick valley and the grey clouds suspended above.

'It's bound to,' he replied, following her gaze, 'this is England.'

She gave him a gentle slap on his knee.

'Do you like living in England?'

'So far I do. I like the people. Some are a bit weird though.'

He looked at her like she was the weird one.

'Do you really think I'm weird? I don't mean to be. I know I'm not like the other girls at school.'

Indigo looked down at her fingers which were busy twisting the ends of her scarf.

'I like weird. Much more interesting. You shouldn't compare yourself to those other girls at school. Why would you want to be like say Georgina or Sophie? They might not be weird but they sure ain't nice. I've seen how they look at some of the other girls and I've overheard them saying things about people. A couple of times I've listened in and it's not very nice.'

'What do they say about me?'

She held her breath, not daring to look up.

'I haven't heard them talk about you.'

'Are you sure? You're not just saying that, are you, because you don't want to hurt my feelings?'

Indigo tried to look him in the eyes but he averted her gaze and looked out of the window.

'Course I'm sure.'

Then she knew he hadn't been telling her the truth. Still she wasn't mad at him. She knew he was only saying that so as not to hurt her feelings. Her mum said that a little white lie - if meant for the right reason - was not a bad thing. She decided not to pursue the conversation.

CHAPTER THIRTEEN

Brandon dragged Indigo into shops she wouldn't normally bother with. Shops selling computer games and sportswear. Still it was fun.

'Come on,' she pulled on his arm, 'I'll show you something you'll like. I bet they don't have this shop in America'

She stopped outside the Science and Nature shop. Brandon's face lit up as he walked in.

'This is awesome.'

His attention was taken by the large telescope at the back of the shop and the books on astronomy. Indigo concentrated on the small animal figures.

'Hey Indigo! Check this out.'

She looked up to see that Brandon had picked up two fluorescent Slinkies and was holding them up to his eyes. Indigo burst out laughing as the metal spirals fell from his eyes to the floor. He looked like a cartoon character.

The shop assistant looked over and scowled.

'Do you mind not doing that? It stretches the coils,' she said, her tone sharp and scolding as she came towards them. Indigo felt her cheeks getting hot. Brandon tried stuffing the Slinkies back in their boxes, fumbling around for what seemed an age as the wiry things refused to go back in the box. The shop assistant saw his difficulty and snatched the boxes off him. Brandon whispered a timid 'sorry', and then motioned to Indigo to leave.

Indigo had been stifling her laugh but when they reached the pavement outside, she couldn't contain herself any longer. It started as a giggle, then Brandon joined in and before long full scale hysteria had set in. Passersby were looking at them as they fell against each other, holding on to their stomachs.

'I can't laugh anymore, my stomach hurts,' Indigo announced in between breaths.

Then she caught Brandon's eye and it all kicked off again. Eventually, the hysteria subsided and they were left with aching jaws and sore stomachs.

It was dark when they walked back to the bus stop. People were beginning to leave work and were hurrying along the streets, buttoning up their coats to keep out the biting wind. As they were walking along one of the streets, close to the cathedral Indigo stopped in mid conversation. She stood there, on the corner, looking concerned.

'What's the matter? Have you lost something?'

Indigo put her hands to her temple.

'I think there's something down there we should take a look at.'

'Like what. There's nothing down there?'

She pointed down a narrow street with lop-sided, sixteenth century buildings overhanging the pavement and shutting out most of the daylight.

'I think there is,' she insisted, pulling him along by his arm.

Most of the shops were boarded up and had long ceased trading. The street had an empty feeling about it, too quiet in stark contrast to the hustle and bustle of the pedestrianised area.

'Here it is,' announced Indigo stopping outside a pet shop.

'Have you been here before?' Brandon queried, raising an eyebrow.

'No…'

'Then how did you…'

Indigo folded her arms and tilted her head to one side and gave him a look.

'Okay. Silly question,' he said, as he realised she was having one of her psychic moments.

Over the shop door the sign read:

'Mr Jacobs. Bespoke Supplier for All Your Pet Needs.'

They looked through the dusty shop window.

That's strange.

It was stocked full of pet supplies; dog and cat food; animal carriers; pet toys but no live animals. Indigo opened the door which activated an old fashioned bell. The smell of damp straw and animal feed filled the air. The shop was dimly lit and it took a few moments for their eyes to get accustomed to the light. The shop was actually quite large with several corridors and doors leading off the main shop area. Large cardboard boxes were stacked high and appeared to hide many nooks and crannies just waiting to be explored.

It's just like a Tardis.

She was like a pet-seeking missile moving down the corridor with quick determination towards a door at the back of the shop. Despite the ringing of the doorbell, no-one had appeared to serve them. On first entering the shop Indigo had noticed a small serving counter with a door behind it. She could see a light coming from the gap in the frame of the door. She had also heard the muffled voice of a man talking on the phone.

'Brandon,' whispered Indigo, 'over here.'

Brandon took a quick look at the serving counter and, confident the shop owner was still talking on the phone, he hurried over to Indigo who was by now trying the handle of the door marked, '*Private. No Access to the Public.*'

'What are you doing?' Brandon hissed back.

She ignored him and pushed the door open.

'Can I help you?'

A man's voice, gruff and hostile called out. They both jumped. Indigo turned to look at him. Hooded eyes looked out from a jaundiced face. He looked like a bird of prey. Indigo shuddered.

'We were just looking for your animals,' blurted Indigo, flustered.

'Can't you read?' he shouted, flaring hawk-like nostrils as he pointed to the sign on the door.

'Sorry. I didn't see that,' she replied.

The man made a move toward Indigo.

'You've no business back here.'

He reached past her to close the door and slammed it shut. She shrank back, chilled by his presence.

This must be Mr Jacobs, the shop owner.

'Do you happen to have any animals here?' asked Brandon, his tone defiant.

'Of course,' Jacobs snapped back, 'this is a pet shop. This way,' he said, as he led them away from the private door.

They followed his stocky frame back down the corridor towards the front of the shop. There was an open doorway that led into a room full of cages. Jacobs pointed to another door beyond that.

'If you're interested in fish you'll find the aquarium through there down the steps in the basement. Confine yourselves to these two rooms in future.'

He turned and marched back to the counter.

'Thank you,' Brandon shouted after him. Spooked by the experience they waited until Jacobs was out of earshot before speaking. As they stood staring at each other they heard the click of a lock.

'He's locked the door marked 'private',' whispered Indigo.

Brandon nodded.

'Let's get out of here. This place gives me the creeps and that guy is seriously weird,' confessed Brandon.

'No. We can't go now. It would look very suspicious.'

Indigo inspected the animals in their cages. They all appeared to be well looked after. The cages were clean and the animals looked healthy. At least that was something. Satisfied that the animals were being cared for, they went downstairs to look at the fish. A dank, wet-fish smell wafted up from the basement.

'Yuk. It stinks down here,' Indigo said, holding her nose.

Despite the awful smell the fish looked well.

'Yeah, let's not stay down here too long. Besides, that guy might decide to lock us in,' Brandon said, peering into a tank of Guppies.

Indigo's imagination had a habit of spiralling out of control and she imagined the two of them imprisoned in the basement, wasting away to nothing, smelling of fish and never being found.

'I think we should go now,' she said, speeding toward the steps.

They hurried back up stairs. This time Jacobs was standing behind the counter, looking watchful.

'Thank you very much,' Indigo said with as much politeness as she could muster.

'Yeah thanks,' added Brandon, followed by a low mutter so that the owner couldn't hear,

'It's been an experience.'

Jacobs said nothing but continued to stare at them until they left the shop.

'I can't see that he does much trade with that attitude. I'm surprised he hasn't been forced to close like the rest of the street,' exclaimed Brandon, who was now in a surly mood.

'He doesn't rely on that side of the business for his livelihood,' announced Indigo with a degree of certainty in her voice.

'Why do I get the feeling that you're going to tell me something I don't know?'

She smiled enigmatically.

'Come on then, I'm waiting…oh psychic one.'

He stopped in the middle of the street, took off his baseball cap and with a flourish bowed down before her. That's what she liked about Brandon. He could always make her laugh.

'Come on. Let's go get some ice cream. I know a great place just round the corner and we can sit down and talk.'

Indigo knew an old-fashioned ice cream parlour run by a kind and jolly Italian. She went there often with her mother and the owner always made a fuss of them.

'*Buon giorno*, Indigo,' he greeted them. 'Where is that beautiful mother of yours today?'

'*Buon giorno*,' she replied in her best Italian accent. 'She's at home.'

'Don't forget to tell her I'm asking after her,' he said, winking at Indigo.

'I won't.'

Indigo didn't know any Italian apart from that one phrase. Brandon looked impressed all the same. They ordered two Italiano specials and sat down.

'Ok. I've waited long enough.'

'Well,' she began, 'I think there's something in that back room that the owner doesn't want anyone to know about.'

'Hold on. Can you start at the beginning? Like how did you know that pet shop was there in the first place?'

'I didn't know. I just got a feeling as we approached the corner of that street. I sensed something and that something told me to go in that direction ...'

'And there it was,' he finished off her sentence.

'Yes. Again I can't be precise but it was the sense of suffering – of an animal in pain.'

'So you think there might be an animal in that room we tried to get into suffering or in pain.' Brandon picked up the menu and studied it, more interested in the food. 'But all those other pets we saw were all well looked after. I saw no signs of mistreatment.'

'I know. That's what's so confusing. But I know what I felt. It was incredibly strong as I approached that door. I just know something is in there.'

'Well, I must admit though that guy was acting seriously strange.'

Their ice cream specials arrived.

'Wow!' exclaimed Brandon.

A huge ice cream sundae, brimming with Italian ice cream, fresh fruit, lashings of chocolate slivers and dark maraschino cherries, was set in front of him and by the look on his face he couldn't wait to tuck in.

'Thought you'd like it. See…you can get decent food in England.'

'Yeah, but that guy is Italian.'

The ice cream held their attention for a while and neither one spoke.

Then Indigo said, 'We need to go back. We need to see inside that room and quick before whatever it is in there disappears.'

'Okay. When? Tonight?'

Indigo smiled. That's what she liked about Brandon. He took her seriously and believed in her. He had never once told her she was just imagining things.

So refreshing.

'It's going to be difficult going back there. He'll be more vigilant. He knows who we are.'

CHAPTER FOURTEEN

The dark nights had closed in and the sudden drop in temperature had brought with it a keen frost, creating a crystallised pattern on the pavement that was slippery underfoot. The street was darker than ever. Most of the street lamps had been smashed which didn't help. They had changed into dark clothing. Brandon's idea. He had such a sense of drama. Actually he was being practical, he said, as it would act as a camouflage. They had decided to walk past the front of the shop to check if they could see any lights on.

'Darn it,' Brandon exclaimed as he noticed the metal shutters had been pulled down in front of the shop window and door preventing them from seeing in. 'Let's go round the back,' he suggested, 'there must be a back way in.'

They walked along the street until they came to a passageway between two buildings.

'This looks like the right direction.'

They hurried along the alley. A central bulkhead light cast their shadows, tall and thin against the brick walls. All they had to do was follow the cobbled street and work out which yard belonged to the pet shop.

'This is it,' whispered Brandon.

Each rear yard was accessible by a double wooden gate, with a wicket gate built in. The name of the shop was clearly painted on the gate. He tried the handle. It was locked.

'What are we going to do now?' he said, a sense of defeat creeping into his voice.

In the distance they could hear the tractor-like sound of a diesel van. Seconds later, the headlights flashed against the wall opposite.

'Quick, hide,' shouted Brandon.

They ran to the wicket gate opposite and tried the handle. It wasn't locked. They stepped in closing it behind them but leaving a small gap to look through. They watched as the van pulled up outside the pet shop. Jacobs got out, unlocked the wicket gate and stepped inside the yard. They waited. Then they heard him unlocking the double gates and watched as he drove his van into the yard. Still watching from their hiding place they saw him struggling with a large cage which he carried out of the van and into the back of the shop. As soon as Jacobs was out of sight Brandon ran across the cobbles and through the open gates with Indigo following close behind. The yard was empty. A noise made them stop. Jacobs was coming back. Brandon spotted some boxes in the corner. He motioned to Indigo and they both made a run for it and ducked behind the stack of boxes. Indigo could feel her heart thumping.

What if he catches us, what would he do to us?

Jacobs climbed back into the van. Brandon reacted fast. He took hold of Indigo's arm, pulled her from their hiding place and ran into the pet shop. Still pulling her, he ran down the corridor and headed for the stack of boxes they had seen earlier that day. They waited and listened, their breathing heavy from their sudden exertion. Jacobs was still outside talking on his mobile phone.

'What shall we do now?' Brandon whispered.

'I need to see inside that room.'

Just at that moment Jacobs hurried back down the corridor. They both tried hard not to breathe or move, peering through the gap in the boxes. He was carrying another cage. He opened the 'private' door. Indigo screwed up her eyes in the hope she would be able to see better and get a glimpse of what was inside the room. It was impossible. Jacobs closed the door behind him. Her heart was thumping louder inside her chest and she felt an urgent need to take a deep breath but knew she couldn't. Her lungs felt like they were going to burst.

How would they get out of this mess now?

The door opened again and Jacobs walked back down the corridor, out into the yard.

'What's he doing?' whispered Brandon.

'I'm not sure but he hasn't locked the door.'

'You're not going to do what I think you're going to do, are you?' an air of resignation in his voice.

'Look, why don't you go to the back door and check out where he is while I go inside and see what's in there.'

'I don't like the sound of this,' he sighed. 'What if he catches you?'

'Trust me. He's not going to come back for a few minutes. It will give me just enough time to confirm what's in there. Go on.'

She pushed him. Brandon went back down the corridor and peered through a window that looked out onto the back yard. He could see Jacobs, smoking and talking on his phone again. Jacobs looked agitated as he paced back and forth.

Indigo took a deep breath as she grasped the door handle with both hands, hoping to make as little noise as possible. The door creaked open and in a flash she was inside the room. The lack of light made it difficult to see but her psychic power brought her attention to a spot behind the door where a cage stood. She tip-toed over to it, sensing the fear of the occupant.

Don't be afraid. I've come to help you.

Staring right at her, with its huge, sad eyes, almost human, was a gorgeous, but frightened, baby Capuchin monkey. She had been right. It was an animal in danger. As she approached, the monkey scurried around in its cage, screeching and grabbing at the bars in a futile attempt to escape. The last thing she wanted was for it to make a noise and bring the shop owner back.

Don't be afraid. All will be well.

Indigo had to work fast. She closed her eyes and placed her hands flat on the bars of the cage.

Time to communicate.

Only minutes had passed before Brandon came rushing back into the room, breaking her flow of concentration. Still, it was enough time.

'Come on. Hurry. He's coming back.'

Indigo opened her eyes. She smiled at the monkey.

I promise. It's going to be all right.

Brandon had stopped in his tracks. 'Yikes. Is that what I think it is?'

'Yes. We'd better go before he comes back.'

They hurried out, closing the door behind them and returned to their hiding place behind the boxes. Jacobs was holding a cool bag this time as he walked back down the corridor. They watched him go back inside the room and close the door behind him.

'Now,' hissed Brandon.

With sleuth-like movements they scudded back down the corridor, out into the yard and through the gates. They turned left and ran down the cobbled street, not once looking behind them. They didn't stop running until they reached the end of the alleyway at which point they turned right and walked towards the end of the street in the opposite direction of the pet shop. Despite being out of breath, they couldn't contain their excitement and between deep inhalations they re-visited the events that had just taken place.

'That was close. I really thought we were going to get caught. But we didn't. That was just awesome. He doesn't even know we were in there.'

He sounded triumphant and very pleased with himself. He continued to babble, gesticulating as he re-lived the moment.

He's having an adrenaline rush.

Indigo, on the other hand, was deep in thought.

Eventually, Brandon's adrenaline rush wore off and he became calmer as he realised he was in a world of his own and Indigo hadn't joined him.

'You're not saying a lot. Are you okay?'

'I'm fine Brandon. I'm just thinking about what the monkey told me.'

'Pardon? Did I hear that correctly? Did you just say the monkey spoke to you?'

The incredulity in his high pitched voice was comical. Perhaps the adrenaline rush hadn't worn off quite yet.

'Well, she didn't exactly speak to me but I was able to communicate with her.'

'Oh wow!' he said, running his hands through his curly hair. 'So you can bring back animals from the dead, you can 'listen in' to other people's conversations and you can talk to animals. A proper little Doctor Doolittle. Anything else I should know about you or are you just going to keep on surprising me?'

'I think I'll keep on surprising you,' she said, breaking into a smile.

She dug into her pocket and pulled out her mobile phone.

'I shouldn't bother with that,' he said with cheerful sarcasm, 'you don't really need it. Just use your 'vibes' to communicate.'

He swept his hands back and forth in front of her face as if he were trying to hypnotise her, making a silly ghost-like sound. Indigo knew he was only having fun and didn't mean any offence. She burst out laughing.

'Come in, whoever you are? This is Monkey Watch to Animal Rescue. Are you receiving me?' he continued to tease.

They were both laughing now releasing some of the tension from a few moments ago. Indigo switched on her phone. The light lit up her face.

'I need to text mum that I'm on my way home otherwise she'll worry about me.'

'I should do the same,' Brandon said, digging into his pocket.

They stood in the unlit street, their mobile phones glowing in the eerie darkness of the night. Brandon could hardly contain himself. His head was buzzing with a thousand questions.

'So what's a monkey doing in the back-room of a pet shop? Why all the secrecy? Why isn't it with the other animals in the shop?' he fired at her.

'She's a Capuchin monkey from the rain-forest in Brazil. I was able to make her understand that we're going to help her and that she has no need to worry.'

Brandon stood open-mouthed. 'Are you for real?'

Indigo ignored him. 'I don't know much more yet but I need to find out quick. They're being handed over to their new owners next Saturday. They need to stabilise them before passing them on.'

'How do you know that?'

'I listened in to his mobile phone conversation when he was in the yard.'

'So you were talking to the monkey and listening in to that guy's phone conversation at the same time?'

'Yeah. You know us girls,' she quipped. 'We multi-task.'

Brandon ignored the mocking comment. 'I suppose you'll be telling me next that you're going to Brazil?'

'Not exactly,' she smiled, not giving anything away.

Brandon suspected she was up to something.

'Does that mean you'll be time travelling like in Star Trek? Or have you got your own time travelling machine, like a Tardis maybe? Can I be the Doctor's Assistant?'

'Oh, be quiet for a minute. I'm concentrating. Don't you take anything seriously?'

'No. I don't think I do.'

'Now, we need to act quickly, they're being moved next Saturday,'

'Hey, that's dad's dinner party.'

'That's not a problem. I should know a lot more by then. I need to speak to someone in Brazil.'

CHAPTER FIFTEEN

Carlos did not like it one bit when his plans went wrong. He detested laziness and incompetence. And those two were turning out to be the laziest and the most incompetent men he had ever had the misfortune to employ. He would catch them drinking and playing cards when they should be out doing business for him. He had recently found a new and cheaper source for his goods and had sent those two idle good for nothings to bring back his lucrative booty. Something they should have done yesterday but instead they chose to get drunk. He would deal with them later.

The boy Chico, however, was a different matter altogether. There was something strange about him. He had seen him often, sleeping underneath old rags and cardboard boxes in the alleyway at the back of the building. There were many boys like him, living rough on the streets and he hadn't taken much notice of him. It wasn't until he watched him intervene in a vicious dog fight one day that his interest was aroused in the boy. The boy appeared to talk to the dogs. His voice alone seemed to have the effect of calming them. From then on Carlos had called him the 'Pet Whisperer'. He realised the boy would be very useful to him, especially in his new line of business. He would have to keep an eye on this boy.

***

The Caatinga rainforest stretched for miles north of Rio de Janeiro. Domingo and Juan had travelled by car most of the way but now, there were no roads for the last leg of their journey. Grumbling, they had abandoned their car and had begun to walk to their final destination, a small village in the heart of the rainforest. Carrying backpacks and machetes they lumbered through the narrow forest tracks, chopping back foliage blocking their path. Domingo, a bull of a man, took the lead, cutting through the dense forest as if it were a sponge cake. Juan followed in his wake. Sweating and irritable from the heat, they made frequent stops to rest and drink their water.

At last, tired and hungry, they came to a small settlement where they were greeted by the children whose excited shrieks announced their arrival. The children took hold of their hands and led them to the village elder, Gael. He was sitting on the ground, cross-legged, under the shade of a pendulous Angico tree surrounded by the village elders, which included Itamar's father. A wiry old man, his teeth all gone, apart from a few at the front that had become no more than yellow and blackened stubs, like spent matches. His eyes, however, had not lost their boyish sparkle. He looked up as the two men approached, greeting them with his toothless grin and inviting them to sit with them.

'Welcome,' Gael said in his native tongue.

Itamar could not help noticing that it wasn't Gael's usual warm greeting.

Ever since his father had told him they were going into the rainforest to capture animals, he couldn't understand why.

It felt wrong to him, so against anything they had ever done before, so disrespectful to the animals. Now he understood. Juan insisted on seeing the animals first. Itamar's father and another man walked over to a wooden hut and brought out two small bamboo cages. In one, perched two magnificent hyacinth macaws, their cyan wings flapping, and their shrill squawking alerting the other animals of danger. The forest was alive with animal panic. In the other cage sat two Capuchin monkeys, mother and baby, clinging on to each other. Oblivious to the fear and suffering of the animals, the two men examined them through the bamboo bars. Satisfied they were in good condition they offered a price.

'Fifty Real for each one?' Juan offered.

Gael nodded his head from side to side.

'Okay, I'll give you seventy five each?'

A heated exchange ensued with lots of haggling. Finally, Juan, chief negotiator, offered Gael one hundred Brazilian Real for each of the animals.

Four hundred Brazilian Real. That is a great amount of money.

Gael, however, was not happy with this offer. He may have looked weak and under-nourished but he was no fool and would not be budged on the price.

'I want two hundred Real for each animal or I will sell to someone else.'

Juan gave Gael an angry look then seemed to get the better of his temper.

'I haven't come all this way to go back empty-handed,' he grumbled to Domingo.

'Me neither. Give the old man his money and let's get out of here.'

Juan turned to the old man. 'We have a deal, old man.'

Gael looked pleased with himself. He stood up and took Juan's hand, holding on to it for longer than was necessary.

'We do business again?'

'You keep catching them, my friend, and we'll keep buying them. But don't go pricing yourself out of the market.'

Gael smiled, showing his crooked teeth. He had done well for the village.

Eight hundred Brazilian Real. Ay yi yi! That is a great deal more money.

He stared as Juan took a large wad of cash out of his pocket and counted it out into Gael's withered hand.

CHAPTER SIXTEEN

Indigo sat on the floor in the candle-lit darkness of her bedroom, her legs crossed. She made an 'O' with her index finger and thumb, resting her hands on her knees. The smoke from her favourite Nag Champa incense curled upwards from an old brass incense holder her mother had given her – another throwback from her hippy days. In several candle holders, tea lights and beeswax candles flickered. She looked up to the dark night sky through her skylight window. Because she lived in a village the light pollution was not quite as bad as in the city or town and she was able to see several magical star constellations. The moon, a bright but thin silver sliver, shone intermittently through the shifting clouds above.

She took a deep breath, filling her lungs and closed her eyes. Focussing on her third eye; that spot just behind the centre of your eyes, she became aware of an intense light, the deep blue of Lapis Lazuli. The feeling was luxurious and uplifting.

She would be entering higher realms of consciousness through doorways leading into other universal dimensions allowing her to connect to the global link up she called 'The Grid'. The grid was a web of psychic communication links surrounding planet earth through which she could communicate with other Indigo children anywhere in the world. She knew who to contact. It was the boy in her dream.

It wasn't clear, even to Indigo children, how they communicated, whether in words, shapes, colours or feelings, but they did. It wasn't long before she had tuned into Itamar's frequency. Indigo explained about her discovery in the pet shop and how the animals were very frightened. In return, he told Indigo about the capture of the monkeys.

'I feel very bad about the monkeys but my family is very poor.'

'I understand, Itamar.'

'And we can make a great deal of money this way. I have seen it.'

'I do understand, Itamar.'

'I feel bad that the animals are suffering but what else can we do? We must accept the wisdom of our elders. I'm sorry but I don't know any more than I have told you. I have no idea what happened to the monkeys or where those men took them.'

She thanked him in his own language of Portuguese and told him she would keep in touch on the grid. In turn he promised Indigo that if he found out any more about the animals he would let her know.

'*Obrigado*, Itamar.'

Emerging from her trance, Indigo sat in the stillness of her room and opened her eyes. She was determined to fit all the puzzle pieces together.

CHAPTER SEVENTEEN

Chico lay asleep on a dirty mattress on the floor of the animal menagerie. The animals were quiet. But not for long. The door opened and in staggered Juan and Domingo. They had been drinking. Walking over to Chico, Domingo kicked him like he was a stray dog in the street.

'Get up.'

Chico leapt up, wiping the sleep from his eyes. He knew only too well the consequences of not obeying Domingo, especially when he was drunk. He had scars on his body from previous beatings. The animals sensed his fear. The macaws high pitched squawking merged with the monkeys piercing screech to deliver a nauseating wall of sound.

'Shut those up.'

Domingo raised his hand to hit Chico but the boy was too quick for him and dodged the blow. He shouted some obscenity at the boy and then slumped down at the table and poured himself a glass of Aguardente. Chico set about soothing the animals. He knew if he didn't get results soon, he would be in for another beating and it would be worse for the animals. Chico hated these evil men. He feared Carlos the most and prayed to be free of them but he knew for him there was no alternative. Only the streets.

Juan watched the boy, fascinated at his way with the animals. Chico moved from one cage to another whispering soothing sounds and touching the animals through the bars of the cage. It was like magic. Each animal looked at him, tilting their heads from side to side as if acknowledging his reassurances. One by one the animals calmed down, some even went back to sleep.

'How does he do that?' he asked Domingo as if Chico were not in the room.

'Beats me. There's something not right about that boy. He gives me the creeps.'

'Oh come on, he's just a boy…'

But this conversation was interrupted when Carlos flew into the room. The two men jumped to attention as if their lives depended on it.

'Where are they?' Carlos demanded.

'In the car, boss. We just got back…'

'Get them in here. Now. We don't have much time.'

Juan and Domingo disappeared and within minutes reappeared in the menagerie carrying two cages, stacked one on top of the other. The two Capuchins and the Macaws.

'Get over here boy and check these animals for me.'

Carlos was the kind of man who never had to ask twice. Chico opened the monkey cage first. Coaxing the animal to him, he lifted her out of the cage. The monkey made little whimpering sounds. She clung to Chico as if he was her own mother making no attempt to escape. Chico examined her. He began with her teeth, opening her mouth and looking inside. He then placed his hands all over her body. The monkey went limp and she closed her eyes.

'She has the end of her tail missing but other than that she is healthy,' he told Carlos, placing the animal back in the cage, where she curled into a ball and went to sleep.

He did the same procedure on each of the animals and pronounced them all well. Carlos seemed pleased for the first time. He instructed the men to put the cages in the back of his pick-up truck.

'You come with me. You two stay here until I come back.'

He tugged on Chico's hair and pulled him outside into the dark and dirty back street. Chico knew where they were going. He had made this trip many times before.

CHAPTER EIGHTEEN

Indigo focused her inner mind and searched the grid once more. It wasn't long before she located Chico. He told her that he was a street boy living in a place called Rocinha, a deprived area of Rio de Janeiro, the capital city of Brazil. Rocinha, he explained, was a ''favela', a very dangerous slum.

'Even the streets have no name and you won't find them on any tourist map,' he informed her, laughing.

How happy this boy is, despite his circumstances.

'I have no family and no home. If I don't do this I will be on the streets begging or running errands for people in exchange for money and food. I don't ask questions. I know they are criminals and what I do is dangerous but I have no option. I must eat.' He told Indigo about Carlos. 'I help him out with the animals in exchange for a bed for the night...'

I'm close to solving the puzzle.

Chico knew that Carlos trafficked animals abroad in return for much more than he paid the villagers who caught them.

'I always do everything he tells me to. I'm afraid of what he will do to me if I don't. I go with him to the airport. The animals are always quiet when I am in the van with them. That's why he takes me with him.'

He told Indigo of the terrible conditions the animals were kept in and the callous treatment they received from Carlos and his gang. Chico was also able to tell Indigo that Carlos had contacts within the airport at Rio, that he had seen him bribing workers there in exchange for false transportation documents.

Indigo thanked Chico for all his help and asked him to stay safe.

***

Indigo came out of her meditative state. She took several deep breaths, exhaled in long, slow breaths, opened her eyes and smiled. The jigsaw puzzle was beginning to come together.

CHAPTER NINETEEN

'Run that past me again?' said Brandon.

They were having one of their conversations where Indigo speed-talks and Brandon listens and tries to understand the weird and wonderful things she tells him. He nearly always asked Indigo to repeat herself, mostly because he could hardly believe what he was hearing. His life had changed so much since meeting her. It was exciting, dangerous, fast paced and utterly unfathomable at times but he wasn't complaining. He loved it and Indigo was just an amazing person to know. He had truly never met anyone like her before. Although what she said was often 'off the wall' she did, paradoxically, make a lot of sense.

'I've been talking to various people on the grid,' she repeated.

'Sorry if I sound dumb but what is the grid? Is it some kind of internet chat room? I haven't heard of it before?'

'I suppose you could call it that,' she laughed, 'but it's a different kind of communication.'

She watched for his reaction, unsure how he would react to this new revelation of her powers.

'And...'

He gestured to her to continue, raising his eyebrows in a resigned fashion. He knew he was about to find out something even more incredible. Indigo explained to Brandon that the grid was a telepathic way of communicating with other children like her anywhere in the world but that it was only possible between like minds. Those on the same wavelength or who resonate with the same vibrational energy.

'So, I'm able to communicate telepathically with other children who are like me.'

'Like a 'mental' search on the Internet?'

'Yes. That's a good way of describing it.'

'After I spoke to Itamar in the rainforest I then spoke to Chico in Rocinha. It's a deprived area in Rio de Janeiro,' she added for clarification, 'He told me about this guy called Carlos da Silva. Anyway,' she sped on, 'he bought the two Capuchins from the village elder and took them back to Rocinha where he runs a back-street animal trafficking business. Anyway, this guy Carlos has contacts with other members of the pet trafficking mafia who provide him with false documents so that he can smuggle them out of the country through the airport in Rio which has this ridiculously long name.'

She rifled through some papers on her desk.

'Here it is. It's called 'Rio de Janeiro Galeao Antonio Carlos Jabim International Airport. What do you think of that?' She had stopped for breath at last. But not for long. 'And that's where we come back to our man Jacobs in the pet shop. He collects the animals from Heathrow airport using false documents and hands them over to customers in this country who pay a lot of money for these animals.'

She drew breath.

'I wonder how much he sells them for in this country,' Brandon asked while he had the chance.

'I'm not sure.'

'Do you think we'd find anything out on the internet?'

Indigo spun round and nudged the mouse. Her Mac monitor flashed into life.

'Let's check it out.'

She typed in the words, 'Capuchin monkeys for sale' into the Google search box. It returned several thousand search results.

'Here we are.'

She clicked on to a site called 'Monkey Business' where lists of exotic animals were openly for sale.

'There,' she said, turning the screen to face him.

Brandon pulled up a chair and peered at the screen.

'Wow! I would never have thought this sort of stuff was just out there for everyone to see.'

'Me neither.'

'It's just like going to the mall and choosing your favourite candy bar. Unbelievable.'

Indigo scrolled through the site. There were several baby monkeys being offered for sale. One in particular caught their eye:

'Three week old, male Olive Baboon. Bottle fed. Diapered. Eating fruits. Prefers Grapes. Spoon fed Fruit Sauces. Pictures available on request.'

'This one's only three weeks old,' Brandon pointed to the screen.

The 'seller' was based in a place called Mission, Texas and their contact details were openly displayed on the site like a classified ad. The 'ad' had been viewed 9,546 times indicating an enormous interest in the trafficking of these animals. He was selling it for 3,000 US dollars.

'Look at this one,' Indigo said, pointing to another monkey on the same site.

'8 week old male, cinnamon Capuchin monkey. Very content, well mannered. This one is selling for 7,000 US dollars'

The seller's location was a place called Bethlehem somewhere in America.

'How much is that in English pounds?' she asked.

'That's about £4,700 at the current rate. Wow! No wonder these guys are getting involved at those prices.'

Indigo scowled. Brandon took no notice and continued, 'So, if the monkeys are sold to the end customer for £3,500 and the profit margin was say, 50% - we need to take off expenses – I imagine there's food, transport costs, various bribes to pay, someone to draw up the false papers. That's still around £1,700 clear profit per monkey.'

'Don't forget the middle man,' Indigo chipped in.

'And Jacobs has two of them in his shop. That's around £3,500 for a few trips to the airport and a few bags of fruit. Easy money,' Brandon continued.

He was biting the end of a pencil when he swivelled round to face Indigo. She wasn't smiling.

'This is serious Brandon. These animals are suffering. They've been taken from their natural habitats, forcibly separated from their mothers. No baby animal should be taken from their mother at three weeks old.'

'I know,' he said, becoming solemn, his tone serious,' but what can we do about it?'

'Not what can we do. What are we going to do is the question. I've been doing a bit more digging on the internet. I did a search on 'pet trafficking'. There are quite a few organisations set up to try and put a stop to illegal smuggling of animals and guess what?'

'What?'

'The most active of them all is a Brazilian organisation called Renctas.'

'I don't suppose it's a coincidence that it's based in Brazil?'

'Did you know pet smuggling is the third largest illegal trade in the world? Illegal drugs and weapons trading are the top two.'

'Wow! That's crazy.'

Indigo started to speed talk again rattling off what she had found out.

'I sent an email to one of them and asked what I should do if I suspected someone of illegal pet trafficking and they told me that they couldn't go into the specifics of how animals were smuggled in and out of countries. I suppose they don't want to give people ideas but they did suggest that we talk to our local Wildlife Crime Officer. I'm not sure what they do and I've never heard of them before but I thought we could go to the police station tomorrow after school and ask to speak to him or her. What do you think?'

'Well, it's nice to be back in the loop again.'

'Sorry Brandon.'

'That's okay,' he said, shrugging his shoulders.

'I didn't deliberately leave you out. It's just that we don't have much time and there are some things that you can't help me with.'

She placed her hand on his arm. 'I couldn't have got this far without you. You were the one who got us into that pet shop. I would never have been brave enough to go in there alone.'

'It just seems like you've leaped ahead of me, that's all. I feel pretty useless.'

'You know I couldn't do this without you.'

He shrugged again but this time it was to shrug off Indigo's compliment. They parted friends agreeing to contact the Wildlife Crime Officer the next day.

CHAPTER TWENTY

The next day after school they cycled over to the local police station. They padlocked their bikes to the railings outside and walked up the concrete steps. A policewoman stood behind the reception counter.

'Can I help you?' she asked, smiling.

'We'd like to speak to the Wildlife Crime Officer if that's possible,' Indigo replied in her best speaking voice.

'Can I ask what it's about?'

'We have some information for him.'

'What sort of information?'

Indigo leaned forward as if she were imparting some important state secret. 'We think we might have come across some pet smuggling.'

'Just one moment. I'll see if he can speak to you now.'

She picked up the telephone next to her and dialled.

'PC Byron?'

There was a pause.

'I have two young people in reception who would like a word with you. Can you come down right away?'

He must have said 'yes' because she replaced the receiver, smiled at them and told them to take a seat and that he would be right down. They couldn't believe their luck. It had been so easy. Indigo had imagined they would have a much trickier task ahead of them, trying to explain who it was they needed to speak to. She was impressed that the policewoman knew what they were talking about. They sat down on some chairs by the window. Uniformed officers walked past them, as they came in and out of the reception area. Indigo was convinced that they were all staring at her, passing judgment upon them.

I bet they think we're petty criminals or vandals, or worse - ASBO candidates.

'Afternoon,' said a uniformed officer.

Brandon nodded like he knew him. Eventually, PC Byron appeared, holding an incident book. 'Hello there, I'm PC Byron, the local WCO. They each gave him a quizzical look. He smiled. 'Sorry, I mean the local Wildlife Crime Officer.'

'Of course,' Brandon replied making out he knew.

He held out his hand to Brandon. Indigo stuffed her hands in her pocket. She wasn't used to shaking people's hands. It didn't seem like the sort of thing she should be doing at her age. He showed them into one of the interview rooms. Indigo warmed to him. He spoke with a soft Irish brogue and had trusting, smiling eyes.

'What can I do for you two today?'

Between them they were able to tell PC Byron what they had stumbled across – the pet shop, Jacobs, the Capuchin.

'How do you know all this?' PC Byron asked.

'I overheard him talking on the phone.'

Indigo lied. She could hardly tell him the real truth. He might think they were a bunch of crazy kids wasting his time.

'The fact is they're being taken to their new owners tomorrow night so something has got to be done before they leave the shop.'

PC Byron listened and made notes.

'What are you going to do?' asked Brandon.

'Well, I'm a firm believer in striking whilst the iron is hot.'

He closed his incident book and stood up. Again, Indigo looked puzzled.

'C'mon. Let's go and pay a visit on Mr Jacobs.'

'Now!' they blurted out in unison.

'Yes. Why not. This way.'

He led them out of the room and outside to a parked police car.

We're going in a police car. How embarrassing.

'Are you getting in?' PC Byron asked her.

She stared at the car as if it had a disease. Again, she noticed people looking at them. She had convinced herself that they really did think she was a juvenile delinquent. She got into the back of the police car before anyone else noticed her. PC Byron shut the door and got behind the driving wheel. PC Byron was the first to speak.

'Have you ever been in a police car before?'

'No. Never,' protested Indigo, not wanting him to get the wrong idea about her.

PC Byron laughed again. 'I didn't mean have you been arrested before or anything like that. I was just making conversation.'

'Oh,' was all she could think to say.

She looked over at Brandon whose gaze was transfixed on the gadgets and displays on the dashboard.

'Is that one of those gizmos that read car number plates and tells you everything about who owns it and whether it's legal and stuff?' Brandon asked.

'ANPR. That's correct. How do you know about those?'

'I watch those cop documentaries on TV. They're awesome.'

PC Byron looked at him in his rear mirror.

'Would you like to be a police officer one day?'

'Maybe. But not in the States. I don't like the idea of getting shot.'

PC Byron didn't answer him but Indigo could see he had a big grin on his face. She listened to their conversation about gadgets and catching criminals until at last, the car turned into the alleyway and pulled up outside the pet shop.

What would Mr Jacobs say when they found the monkey? What would he do? Would he try to escape?

Indigo's stomach felt like it had an army of butterflies fluttering inside it. Her thoughts were frantic too.

PC Byron opened the door, activating the old-fashioned bell. Brandon and Indigo followed him, keeping close. Jacobs was stood behind the counter talking on his mobile phone. He looked up.

'Have to go now. I have customers.'

He put the phone back in his pocket.

'Can I help you officer?'

'Sorry to trouble you, sir, but it's come to my attention that there may be some illegal pets on your premises. Would you mind letting me have a look around.'

'Someone 'bin pulling your leg, officer?'

Jacobs looked straight at Indigo. She shuddered.

'Weren't you two in here yesterday afternoon?'

'Yes. We were,' Brandon answered.

'What tales have you been telling this policeman? Don't you know it's a crime to waste police time?'

'If you wouldn't mind, sir? It won't take a minute and then we'll be on our way.'

'Of course, officer. I don't mind at all. Where would you like to start?'

'Where did you say you saw the animals?' PC Byron asked Indigo.

'They were down that corridor in a room marked 'private'.'

She glanced at Jacobs to see his reaction. He looked surprised but not unduly worried.

'That room is always locked. I fail to see how you would have seen any animals in there, let alone one that was illegal.'

'Nevertheless, would you mind opening it for us?' PC Byron persisted.

'Certainly officer.'

Got him now. How's he going to get out of this?

He took a set of keys out of his pocket and walked in front of Indigo. Jacobs unlocked the door and pushed it open for the group to go inside. The cage had gone.

'What have you done with it?' Indigo challenged.

'Done with what?'

'The monkey?'

'I don't know what you're talking about. Don't you think this has gone far enough officer?'

He turned towards PC Byron, holding his hands in the air.

'Sorry to have disturbed you, sir. We'll be on our way now. Thank you for your time. You've been very understanding.'

He started to walk out of the room.

'Is that it?' Brandon asked, 'Aren't you going to search the rest of the place?'

PC Byron stopped.

'I think we've taken up enough of this gentlemen's time. Let's go. Before I get accused of police harassment,' he joked.

Jacobs laughed. Indigo's concern turned to desperation.

'But there was a monkey here. He must have done something with it?'

She took one last look around the room. There was nothing. It was completely empty. There was nowhere he could have hidden the cage.

'I think you'd better go before you both get arrested for wasting police time,' Jacobs suggested.

Indigo left the shop. Inside the car she asked PC Byron if he believed them.

'I have to look into all allegations of pet smuggling. It's a dangerous business with some very dodgy characters involved so you can't be too careful. But without any evidence there's nothing I can do. I will keep an eye on our Mr Jacobs though.'

Indigo sat in silence all the way back.

There must be some explanation. Those monkeys can't just disappear into thin air.

As they got out of the car PC Byron thanked them for bringing the pet shop to his attention and said he would be in touch if anything came up regarding Mr Jacobs' activities. They stood outside the police station, pulling on coats and wrapping scarves around their necks. It was already dark.

'I don't get a good feeling about this...' Indigo began.

'Yeah. I've got that feeling too. But where does that leave us?'

'I don't know but we have to find out where those monkeys are. We can't just let this happen. We have to do something.'

Demelza spent a long time getting ready for Luke's dinner party. Indigo watched her mother as she tried on one dress, then another.

'How does this look?'

'You look gorgeous mum,' she reassured her.

'Hmmn. I'm not sure,' she replied diving back into her wardrobe and flicking through her clothes.

'I don't think it gives quite the right message.'

'And what message might that be?'

'Oh, you know, sophisticated but different.'

Demelza laughed. 'I can do different, that's easy. But I'm not sure about sophisticated.'

Indigo picked up her mother's jewellery box and sat down on the bed. She rifled through its contents, picking up a necklace or a bangle and holding them up to her mother. Demelza shook her head at Indigo's choices.

'You like Luke, don't you mum?' She didn't wait for her reply. 'I think you do.'

She turned to Indigo. 'I do like him. Is that okay with you?'

'It's fine mum. I think it's great.'

'You do?'

'Yeah. I think he's really nice.'

Crazy thoughts, like whether her mother would marry Luke started whirling in her head. That would mean Luke would become her step-dad and Brandon her step-brother.

How weird was that?

'I think Brandon's really nice too.'

'Mum,' she protested, 'he's just a friend.'

'I know. I'm just saying I like him. He has a nice mind.'

'Are you feeling a bit nervous about tonight mum?'

'I am a bit.'

'Well you look fantastic.'

Demelza finally chose a tight fitted, ankle length, green dress. The colour of her dress contrasted perfectly with her hair which she had left flowing free, revealing the white flesh of her back through a diaphanous shrug. She looked more bo-ho than pre-raphaelite tonight thought Indigo. Definitely not hippy.

'Love the shoes, mum.'

Demelza looked down at her high heels and the glittering green toe varnish.

'I just hope I can walk in them.'

'You'll certainly give them all something to talk about tonight.'

'I know. That's what I'm afraid of.'

Demelza picked up her clutch bag and took one last look in the mirror.

'You'll be late.'

Indigo thought her mother would never leave. She watched her as she glided out to the waiting taxi in her high heels, her dress fluttering in the wind and waited till the taxi drove away before calling Brandon.

Everything was still going according to plan. Earlier that day Indigo and Brandon had sketched out a vague modus operandi. They had agreed not to say anything to their parents about the pet shop or what their intentions were.

'They'll be too busy with their dinner party,' Brandon had re-assured her.

The vague plan was that Brandon would sneak out during the dinner party, ride his bike over to Indigo's house and set off for the pet shop. They had both decided that they couldn't allow Jacobs to get away with his plans to sell the monkey. Their precise plan as to how they were going to achieve this had not been thought out. They had decided to 'wing it'.

Indigo was pacing up and down in her bedroom, looking out of the window every five minutes. She couldn't wait to get to the pet shop and was worried they'd be too late to rescue the monkeys.

What on earth is keeping him?

Then she saw him, pedalling fast down the road towards the house. She grabbed her coat and ran downstairs.

'Sorry I'm so late.' Brandon apologized, catching his breath. 'I couldn't get away any sooner.'

'That's okay. Mum hasn't been gone long. Come on let's get going.'

'We might be too late,' Brandon suggested.

They jumped onto their bikes and pedalled into the dark.

As they approached the pet shop they could not be sure if anyone was there. From the rear of the building it was difficult to see any lights. They left their bikes behind the gate of the yard opposite and tip toed across the cobbles to the pet shop's wicket gate. Brandon tried the brass handle. It made a grating noise as it turned. He pushed the door and peered through the crack.

'Someone is here,' he whispered.

Brandon pushed open the gate and stepped into the yard. The van was there with the back doors open. No sign of anyone.

'Quick, let's get behind those boxes.'

They made a dash for it and hid behind the same stack of boxes and waited. After a few moments, Jacobs appeared carrying the monkey.

Poor thing. She looks frightened.

He lifted the cage into the back of the van then disappeared inside the shop again.

This is our chance. I knew it.

They ran towards the back of the van and looked in. The inside had been customised. Wooden shelves lined the walls on both sides, fitted with fastenings to hold the cages in place. Thick curtains had been fitted to the bottom of the shelves along their full length. They climbed inside and took a quick peep under the curtains. Nothing there.

Where has he put the monkey?

It was then they both heard Jacobs coming back out of the shop. Indigo motioned Brandon to get out of the van. Instead of jumping out he grabbed hold of her and pushed her under the curtain. He then dived across the van and hid behind the curtain on the other side. They both lay there trying to control their breathing as Jacobs climbed back into the van. Indigo was so close she could hear his chest wheezing as he struggled with his contraband.

That would be the smoking.

Although she could see nothing she was aware he was holding another cage. Indigo lifted the edge of the curtain. Inside were two capuchin monkeys. Mother and baby.

So that's where he hides them. In a false cupboard at the back of the van.

Jacobs closed the door, jumped out of the van with a thud, slammed it shut and locked the van doors. Indigo lay there in the cold blackness. She lifted the curtain up to look across at Brandon. She couldn't see a thing.

'He's started the engine. What are we going to do?' she whispered into the blackness.

'There's not much we can do. Are you okay?' Brandon whispered back.

'Sort of. You?'

'I'm fine.'

'Did you see the other cage?'

'There's more than one?'

'He must have had another delivery. It's a female Capuchin with her baby. He's hidden them in a false cupboard.'

'Listen…when he stops the van, we'll wait till he offloads the first cage, then I'll turn on my phone and call 999. He'll be caught red handed then and that should be enough proof for the police. Okay?'

'Okay. Sounds good.'

They spent the rest of the journey in silence, not daring to speak in case Jacobs heard them. The animals were also quiet.

Why are they so quiet?

At first Brandon could hear other traffic noises as they passed through Gloucester, then the van speeded up. He guessed that they were on a dual carriageway by the speed. After some time, the van slowed down and took a right turn. Brandon tried to memorise every turn. He would need to if he was going to help the police find them. A sharp left turn followed and they were being bumped along a dirt track.

'Sounds like we're going down a country lane,' Brandon whispered.

He was right. After a few more minutes of being bumped around on the hard floor the van came to a stop. They heard Jacobs get out and come round to the back of the van. Someone else joined him. Indigo could hear muffled voices coming from outside. Then the doors opened.

Please don't look behind the curtains.

Then someone climbed into the van. She could see their boots through the gap beneath the curtain. It was Jacobs. She heard him unscrew the false back, heard him curse as he struggled to remove the metal cage from its hiding place, then clamber back out leaving the van doors open.

Still no sound from the monkeys.

An outside light from what looked like an outbuilding offered some illumination and they were able to see from their hiding places. They watched as Jacobs, now joined by a much taller man, walked towards the outbuilding and disappeared inside. Brandon scrambled from underneath the curtain and jumped out of the van. Indigo followed. She looked over at the outbuilding where the two men were talking and let out an audible intake of breath.

'Oh my Goddess!'

'What's the matter?'

'This is Georgina's house.'

Brandon pulled out his phone and turned it on. The light from the phone seemed incredibly bright. Brandon covered it with his hand in case it caught the attention of the smugglers. Micro seconds later, Indigo heard the annoying and very irritating 'welcome' tune.

'Switch it to silent mode,' she hissed at him.

'I can't. The sim card isn't ready.'

Too late. Jacobs had heard it and was running towards them, followed swiftly by the tall figure.

'Who's that?' shouted Jacobs, 'What the blazes are you doing here?'

It all happened so quickly. The light; the stupid tune; the man running and shouting at them. There was no time to escape. The tall figure, whom Indigo now recognised as Georgina's father, Mr Ash, grabbed hold of Brandon, while Jacobs made a grab for Indigo. Holding on to her with a vice-like grip Jacobs took out a Maglite from his pocket and shone it into her face. She felt like a rabbit caught in the headlights, too frozen to struggle. Brandon was much taller and strong for his age. He struggled with Ash and almost got free until Jacobs threatened to knock Indigo out. Then he stopped struggling.

'Get them inside quickly,' Jacobs shouted.

'Now look here. Wait a minute,' Ash protested.

Brandon thought his accent very plummy, like the character Doctor Watson in Sherlock Holmes. Brandon was waiting for him to say something like 'This whole thing is preposterous' or something like it.

'What are you going to do?'

'Just shut up and get them inside,' Jacobs shouted.

They were frog-marched to the out building. The door shut behind them. The inside smelled like an old garden shed and its contents were not too dissimilar. An old lawnmower was stacked in a corner along with various gardening implements.

'Now look here,' began Ash, 'I wasn't expecting anything like this. I thought we had a straightforward business deal?'

He stood tall, puffing out his chest in an attempt to appear threatening.

Brandon was not convinced. Nor was Jacobs.

'I hadn't bargained on this either. I ain't exactly pleased myself.'

He turned an angry face towards Brandon and Indigo. 'What are you two doing here on this gentleman's property? It's trespassing you know.'

'And that's illegal pet smuggling,' shouted Indigo pointing at the cage that had been placed on a table in the middle of the room. She could see the baby Capuchin now. It was lying limp inside the cage, lifeless.

Please be well.

'What are you talking about?' Jacobs snarled.

'Never mind. What matters is the police will be here any minute. I've already spoken to them and they're on their way,' Brandon bluffed.

Jacobs snatched the phone from his hand and pressed the green button. 'According to this it says the last person you rang is someone who goes by the name of 'Indigo'. Who's that?'

Brandon looked at Indigo. It was an instinctive reaction.

'I see. So you're Indigo? Then we don't have to worry 'cos you're here and it looks like the police aren't coming after all 'cos they don't know where you are,' he sneered. He turned to Indigo. 'Give me your phone?'

She dug into her pocket and gave him her iPhone. It was still switched off. He pressed the top button. The light came on, followed by the vibrating message tone.

'You've got a message.' He slid his finger across the screen. 'It's from "mummy". It says, 'Worried about you. It's late. Where are you?' Well that's even better. He hasn't phoned the police and looks like nobody knows where you are.'

He sneered at them both.

'This whole situation is getting totally out of hand. It's utterly preposterous,' interrupted Ash.

Brandon burst out laughing. He whispered to Indigo.

'Is this guy for real or did someone hire him for the night?'

'You think it's funny?' Jacobs spat out the words with menacing intent.

'Excuse me Mr Jacobs?' Indigo said. He swung round to face her. 'What do you intend to do with us?'

'I haven't decided yet.'

Indigo's approach seemed to have thrown him off course. He seemed calmer.

'Well, I was just thinking. At the moment you're only guilty of pet smuggling – although personally I think that is a serious crime – but it isn't as serious as holding us against our will…or worse?'

Ash threw his arms in the air. He plodded towards Jacobs, his green wellingtons squeaking across the flagged floor.

'Look here. I'm not standing for any more of this nonsense. I want you all off my land now. I want nothing more to do with this. And you can take that thing away with you,' he pointed to the cage, 'I knew I should never have let my wife talk me into this.'

'What about my money?' Jacobs demanded, 'we had a deal?'

'Forget your money. The deal's off. Just get out of here.'

He 'shooed' Jacobs towards the door.

'We had a deal,' Jacobs shouted back.

It was either the thought of not getting his money or the insult of being 'shooed out' of the building that made Jacobs see red. He rushed at Mr Ash, knocking his flat cap from his head. Ash bent down to pick it up, Jacobs brought his knee up and kneed Ash in the chin. As Ash straightened himself, Jacobs swung a surprise punch to his stomach, momentarily knocking the air from his lungs. This was rapidly followed by a jab to his face. Smack. Ash cried out in pain. Indigo winced at the noise of hard knuckles connecting with bone. Jacobs landed several more punches at Ash. His face was smeared with blood coming from his nose and a gash above one of his eyes. Appearing to forget Brandon and Indigo were in the room, and focusing all his attention on Ash, Jacobs pummelled Ash like a man possessed. Brandon edged towards the door indicating to Indigo to do the same.

The fight was in full swing now with garden furniture hurtling across the room as the two men pushed and punched each other. They fell against the table. Tipping it over. The cage crashed to the floor. Indigo stifled the impulse to run and catch hold of it. They continued to edge toward the exit. Brandon was near the door now, his back to it. He fumbled for the handle and found it.

'Run for it,' he shouted, pushing the door wide open. 'Just keep running.'

They were side by side running toward the farm track they had driven down earlier. Indigo's lungs were burning with the cold air. Brandon took a quick look behind him and saw Jacobs' heavy frame lumbering after them, gaining on them.

'He's coming after us.'

He took hold of Indigo's hand, pulling her along faster. Indigo's foot struck a rock. Wham. She felt her hand being ripped out of his as she slammed onto the frost hardened ground. The cold air flew from her lungs as she lay there stunned watching Brandon run on not realising she had fallen. Then he stopped and turned.

'Keep going, don't stop,' she screamed.

She heard Jacobs' quick footsteps behind her, coming ever closer.

'Got you, now,' he roared, as he made a grab for her.

She could hear his chest making a hollow, rasping sound as he breathed and could smell tobacco on his breath. With no strength left to fight him off, she lay still. Then everything changed. With unexpected suddenness, she was confronted by a row of bright lights. Piercing sirens. Screeching tyres. Blinding headlights.

There were cars everywhere. Several uniformed police officers appeared. Two of them ran towards Jacobs and rugby tackled him to the frozen ground. The others ran towards the outbuilding. Four people emerged from the car in front. Two uniformed and two others. Indigo recognised her mother.

'Mum,' she breathed, still winded.

She managed to pick herself up and despite the aching in her lungs run as fast as her legs would take her towards her mother. When she reached her she almost knocked her to the ground.

'Are you okay? Has anyone hurt you?'

'I'm fine mum. Honestly.'

She turned to see Luke hugging Brandon.

'Gee, am I pleased to see you,' Brandon said.

He looked relieved to see his father.

'But how did you know we were here?'

'That was easy,' he said, letting go of his son. 'Have you forgotten your mobile phone has a tracking device in it? When it got to midnight, we both started to get really worried so we rang the police. They were able to track your location using the tracking device.'

Indigo looked up to the star lit sky and mimed a silent 'thank you' to the Universe.

Demelza copied her daughter. Luke and Brandon looked on at this strange behaviour. Then they all laughed. It had the advantage of breaking the tension they all felt. Still hugging each other they watched as Jacobs was bundled into the back of a police car. Ash emerged from the outbuilding looking dishevelled and protesting in a loud and pompous manner as the police officers led him away. As they stood there another car came towards them from behind the outbuilding. It was Mrs Ash driving her four-by-four in an erratic fashion. She must have seen the police cars because she attempted to do a three-point turn to get away. The police, however, had other plans for her.

A policewoman ran to the front of the car and held up her warrant card.

'Stop. Police,' she shouted, while another approached the driver's side.

Mrs Ash stopped the car and turned off her engine. As she got out of the car Mr Ash started hurling abuse at her.

'You stupid woman,' he began.

'Oh, for goodness sake. Just shut up, will you,' she slurred back.

'Look what you've got me into. I told you not to spoil that child. I knew no good would come of it.'

'Have you been drinking, Madam?' asked the policewoman.

'Of course I have.' Mrs Ash shouted back.

The policewoman took the keys from the ignition.

Oops. That's another reason to arrest her.

Mr and Mrs Ash were still bickering at each other as the police drove them away. Indigo insisted on going back into the outbuilding to check on the Capuchin. A policeman had already opened the cage and was peering inside at the monkey who lay lifeless.

'Is she dead?' asked Indigo.

'I can't say. Don't really have much to do with monkeys in my line of work.' Noticing her concern, he added, 'I've sent for the police vet and PC Byron, our Wildlife Crime Officer. Don't worry, she'll be well looked after now. It's best you go on home and get some rest. I'll see the squad car takes you.'

'What about the others?'

'What others?'

'There's another one in the back of the van.'

'We've already looked in there.'

'There's a hidden cupboard at the back,' Brandon informed him.

The policeman looked startled.

'We saw him put the cage in there earlier.'

They went back outside to find them. The police officer climbed into the van, followed by Brandon and Indigo. Brandon showed the officer the false back. He slid the panel along to reveal an airless and confined space. The cage was in darkness.

'I can't see anything in here.'

Brandon noticed a torch clipped to the inside of the van.

'Here. Use this.'

The policeman shone the torch inside the cupboard. There was the cage. Indigo hurried out of the van. Her senses told her there was something wrong. As they were making their way back into the outbuilding, a small van pulled up outside, making a harsh crunching noise on the gravel. Indigo turned to see the police vet emerge from her van.

Please let her be in time.

They placed the cage containing mother and baby on the table and Indigo got her first proper look. Neither monkey showed any signs of life. The mother lay in a fetal position, her baby snuggled in close. The vet lifted the tiny form away from its mother. The mother did not stir even as she was being separated from her baby.

The vet took out her stethoscope and placed it on the mother's chest. Indigo, Brandon, Luke, Demelza and the police officer looked on in silence. Indigo held her breath and tightened her grip on her mother's hand. The vet said nothing. After several seconds, she took the stethoscope out of her ears and wrapped it around her neck.

'She's gone.'

A soul chilling cry cracked the silence.

'No, no,' Indigo cried, sobbing and shaking, 'it can't be.'

'Can't you do something?' Brandon implored, looking at Indigo.

'It's too late,' Indigo sobbed, shaking her head.

'What about the baby?' Brandon asked.

The vet placed her stethoscope on the lifeless, tiny chest of the baby.

'This one's still alive.'

She dug into her vet bag and pulled out a small syringe which she filled from a thin vial and, feeling for a muscle, injected the patient. Next she took out a thermal blanket which she put over the baby Capuchin.

'There's another one over there,' the policeman pointed out, his voice hesitant, as he feared the worst.

The vet picked up her stethoscope and listened for the baby's heart. She turned to Indigo. 'I'm sorry.'

Indigo broke down. Her mother put her arm around her. 'I want to go home,' she said in between deep sobs.

'We're going now, darling,' soothed her mother, guiding her out of the building.

CHAPTER TWENTY TWO

That night Indigo's dreams were full of animals in pain and of her being chased down long corridors by evil men. When she woke she felt as exhausted as when she went to bed. Her waking thoughts were of the baby Capuchin and whether she had recovered. She crawled out of bed and put on her leopard slippers - another donation to the WWF. She padded downstairs to the kitchen and was surprised to see Luke and Brandon sitting at the kitchen table. Brandon was sipping juice and mum and Luke were drinking coffee.

'Oh hi,' she greeted them, rubbing the sleep from eyes. 'What are you doing here?'

'Morning darling.' Demelza stood up. 'We didn't want to wake you. How are you feeling?'

'Tired still. I didn't sleep well. Had bad dreams.'

Demelza walked over to the fridge and poured out some juice. Indigo sat down at the table.

'Someone called PC Byron rang this morning. He said he wanted to come over later today to see both of you. So I rang Luke and invited them over for coffee. Brandon's been filling us in on Mr Jacobs and the pet shop.'

'Did he say anything about the monkey?'

'No. Sorry. I didn't think to ask.'

'That's okay mum.'

They sat chatting for a while and then Demelza suggested it was about time that Indigo got dressed. PC Byron arrived just as Indigo was making her way back downstairs. Demelza was showing him into the lounge. She ran into the room after them. PC Byron was about to perch himself on the edge of a voluminous sofa that was more like a bed than anything else.

She couldn't wait to find out and dismissing the usual mode of greeting, fired questions at PC Byron. 'Is the monkey okay?' Where is she? What's going to happen to her?'

'Hello there,' he replied, eyes smiling.

'Indigo! Let PC Byron at least sit down before you interrogate him,' her mother chided.

Indigo sat down next to Brandon on the opposite, equally engulfing, sofa.

'She's fine, absolutely fine. No need to worry there. But I'll get to that in a minute, if that's okay. Before I say anything, I'd just like to apologise. I must confess I didn't take either of you seriously after the visit to the pet shop.'

Indigo and Brandon flashed each other a look.

I knew you didn't.

PC Byron coughed. 'Well, I thought it only fair to come and see you both and let you know what has happened since last night. Mr

Jacobs has made a partial confession. It all fits in with what you told me at the police station but we still don't know who his contacts are abroad. Mr Ash has also been co-operative. I'm afraid I can't say the same for Mrs Ash.

'That's no surprise given her behaviour on the night,' said Luke.

'Quite. Well, according to Mr Ash, his wife bought the Capuchin as a birthday gift for his daughter. He says he didn't realise she was doing anything illegal. I think he probably did but that's irrelevant now. I got the feeling he didn't approve of such an expensive gift, that perhaps she was spoiling his daughter.'

'That figures,' quipped Luke.

'When we interviewed Mrs Ash she claimed not to know anything about it. Claimed not to know Mr Jacobs. Tried to blame it all on her husband. But as I said Mr Jacobs has been very forthcoming. He confirmed the only person he had dealt with was Mrs Ash until last night. I have a feeling she may want to change her story.'

'What will happen to them?' asked Luke.

Everyone stared at PC Byron.

'They'll probably be charged with illegal smuggling of animals. Could be looking at a prison sentence?'

'Prison?'

Brandon who had been quiet up till now appeared shocked.

'Yes, young man. Pet smuggling is a serious business.'

'And Mr Jacobs? Will he go to prison?' asked Brandon.

'He's definitely looking at a custodial sentence. Looks like he's been trafficking illegal animals for some years. Probably looking at fifteen years and upwards.'

'Wow!' Brandon exclaimed, as he ran his hand through his hair, 'That's some sentence.'

'It's only what they deserve,' Demelza offered. 'Call it Karma.'

'Karma?'

Brandon looked puzzled.

'What goes around, comes around,' Indigo added, 'Mum believes that if you behave badly towards people, you might get away with it once or twice or even for a long time but eventually the Universe returns to you what you give out to others, three fold.'

'You mean like 'Pay Back Time' with interest?'

Demelza threw her head back and laughed. 'You could call it that,'

Everyone burst out laughing at Brandon's interpretation of Karma. Indigo could tell that Brandon was still a novice on the path to enlightenment. More concerned about the animal suffering caused than the human cost of trafficking she turned her attention to the surviving monkey.

'So what's happened to the monkey? Where is she now?'

'I arrived just after you left. The vet was still examining her. She confirmed that she had probably been given something to make her sleep. She checked her out and re-assured me that she was fine. She thinks the mother may have had too large a dose which is why she didn't make it.'

'And the other baby?'

'According to the vet, she was too young to be taken away from her mother. She died from dehydration as a result of not having the proper food.'

Everyone looked at Indigo, expecting her to get upset again.

'It's okay. I'm fine now.'

'You'll be happy to know that she's been taken to the monkey sanctuary to be looked after in the short term…'

'What monkey sanctuary?' asked Brandon.

'It's a rescue centre for monkeys and apes based in Wales. They rescue monkeys from zoos and laboratories. They provide a home for them. She'll be with other monkeys and well looked after. That's what I came to see you about. Would you like to visit?'

'Yes! Yes, please. When? When can we go?' she cried, jumping up, so excited she didn't let PC Byron finish his sentence.

'Next weekend if that's all right with your parents?'

'Mum,' pleaded Indigo with puppy dog eyes, looking over at her mother.

'It's okay with me?' Demelza answered, looking over at Luke for his approval.

'Dad?'

'I suppose it'd be okay.'

'Yes!' they both raised their hands and gave each other an enthusiastic high five.

PC Byron struggled out of the sofa.

'Before you go...' began Indigo. 'Did Mr Jacobs mention a man named Carlos?'

'No. Who is he?'

Indigo had to think fast.

'It's just I'm sure I heard that name mentioned when he was talking on the phone. Something about Brazil?'

'He hasn't mentioned that name but I will ask him. Brazil is a known source for pet trafficking. It would be good if we could find the source but it's extremely difficult. I've been doing this job for several years now and I've yet to see anyone successfully convicted. But I'm really confident about this case. Thanks to you two. I won't keep you any longer. I have endless paperwork to catch up on now. But I'll see you next week.'

'Sure thing.' Brandon quipped.

Luke stood up and offered his hand. 'Thank you PC Byron. Appreciate you coming round to see the children.'

When PC Byron had gone they all sat back in the lounge.

'Well done Indigo. It's amazing. You seem to have achieved more in a few days than PC Byron has done in his whole career. How did you do it?' Luke asked.

Brandon looked at Indigo then back at his dad.

'Don't ask dad. Don't go there.'

PC Byron kept his word. He arrived to collect them as promised. Indigo was so dreading he would turn up in a police car and was relieved when he pulled up outside her house in an unmarked people carrier. She hadn't been able to sleep the night before she was so excited about going to monkey sanctuary and seeing the baby Capuchin again.

On the way there, PC Byron gave them an update on Jacobs and Mr and Mrs Ash. Jacobs had been surprisingly co-operative and had told them all he knew. Indigo wanted to know if he had found anything out about Carlos in Rio but PC Byron had drawn a total blank. Mrs Ash, on the other hand, had continued to be completely un-co-operative. She still denied all knowledge of the monkey and said it was all her husband's idea. Mr Ash blamed it all on his wife saying he was only doing her a favour by meeting Jacobs on the night in question.

Poor old Mr Ash.

He claimed he had no idea that Jacobs was going to hand over an illegal monkey to him.

And what of Georgina?

Indigo had been at school all week with no sign of Georgina. No-one had seen her and the official line from school was that she was ill.

PC Byron explained that Georgina had been taken to her grandparents as Mr and Mrs Ash had been kept in custody.

Poor Georgina.

Indigo remembered all the times Georgina had tormented her, laughed at her and called her a loser. There had been countless times she had wished Georgina would leave school. But now she might have to leave school altogether. She couldn't help feeling sorry for her. It was bad enough having a mother like Mrs Ash.

When they arrived at the centre they were greeted like VIPs. Juliet, the Head Keeper, explained the day's events. They were to be allowed into the monkey's enclosure to help clean out the rotting fruit skins and bring them fresh fruit.

This was truly an honour as only the animal keepers were ever allowed into the enclosures. They gathered up the equipment they would need, buckets, rubber gloves and followed Juliet to the enclosure. Indigo spotted the rescued baby Capuchin and the Capuchin appeared to recognize her. The monkey swung across the wooden branches, landing on Indigo's shoulders.

'She knows who I am!'

Indigo couldn't hide her delight. She talked to the monkey in the same way Brandon had seen her talk to her pets at home. The monkey looked at Indigo with wise eyes. It seemed to understand her every word.

'You certainly have a way with animals,' Juliet commented as she collected half-eaten scraps of food from the ground.

'You can say that again,' Brandon said, making himself useful and throwing banana skins into his bucket. 'You should see her bedroom back home. It's wall to wall with cages of animals.'

Juliet stopped and stood up, a look of surprise on her face. 'You keep animals in cages?'

Indigo's smile turned to puzzlement. 'Yes. Is there something wrong in that?'

'Sorry. I sometimes react too quickly. I can be very judgmental when it comes to animals.'

The monkeys were jumping from one branch to another getting ever closer and giving fruit skins. Juliet had not given her an answer and the atmosphere had turned tense. It was as if something were hanging there between them all. Something unsaid. Indigo broke the silence.

'Do you think it's cruel to keep animals in cages?'

Juliet carried on clearing up this time, aware that the monkeys were getting impatient to be fed. 'My philosophy is that all animals should be allowed to live in their natural habitats.'

Indigo needed further clarification. 'Even if they're captive bred?'

Brandon remembered her saying it was all right to keep animals in cages as long as they were captive bred when he had questioned her in her bedroom and he was eager to see how this conversation would go.

'Being raised captive bred is unnatural. It's not natural to raise animals in captivity. Full stop. Just like it wouldn't be natural to raise humans in captivity. But somehow we seem to be able to justify it to ourselves. We think it's okay because it's only animals and our desire to have them overrides our logic.

Indigo could feel her face burn red with shame. Juliet had hit a nerve. It was true. She could see now, watching the monkeys running around in the large enclosure how wrong she had been. She looked across at the baby Capuchin. What a difference to the last time she saw her, lying half dead in a small cage.

How selfish I've been.

She shuddered with the shame. She could see now how she had justified it to herself. Juliet walked over to Indigo and placed her arm around her.

'Are you all right? I didn't mean to upset you. I can be too outspoken. My friends tell me that all the time.'

She laughed trying to make Indigo feel more relaxed.

'I have a surprise for you. Maybe now is a good time?'

'A surprise?' queried Indigo.

'We haven't chosen a name for your monkey yet. We thought you might like to?'

Indigo's expression changed.

'Would I? Oh, I would love to.'

She searched the animal's enclosure, looking for inspiration. A dried out mango skin lay on the ground. Indigo's eyes brightened and she became her excited self again. 'Mango. How about naming her Mango?'

Juliet seemed pleased with her choice.

'That really suits her. Good name.'

The rest of the day was truly magical and the cloud of their earlier conversation had lifted but the best was yet to come. As they got ready to leave, Juliet stopped them.

'Oh, I nearly forgot. One last surprise.'

'Another surprise? Wow! This day just keeps getting better,' Brandon exclaimed, wondering what the surprise could possibly be.

Brandon and Indigo listened as she explained to them that after several months the Capuchin would be ready to be re-introduced into the Brazilian rainforest.

'Would you be interested in accompanying them to Brazil?'

Would we be interested in joining them in Brazil? Is the sky blue?

Indigo's stomach did several somersaults.

'Are you serious?' Brandon asked.

'Never more.' Juliet held out her arms in a gesture of exasperation as if she couldn't really believe their hesitation. 'Well...'

'I'd have to ask dad,' cautioned Brandon.

'That's okay,' said Juliet, 'we've already checked with your parents - they think it's a great idea.'

Indigo could not believe what she was hearing. It was like a dream. Being invited to the sanctuary was one thing – but Brazil.

'I'm going to Brazil. I'm going to the Rainforest,' she said, jumping up and down and clapping her hands like an over-wound toy.

CHAPTER TWENTY FOUR

It seemed like an eternity to Indigo before the time came to travel to Brazil. The summer holidays had arrived and everything had been arranged for their trip. The evening before her departure she was sitting cross-legged on her bedroom floor, meditating to calm her pre-flight nerves when she became aware of Chico tuning in on the grid.

Something was wrong.

He was in trouble. She could sense his fear but it was so intense he was blocking their energy field, making it difficult for her to communicate with any clarity. She placed all her concentration on the messages coming through but they were hopelessly garbled.

'Help me Indigo. I need help...'

Then nothing. It was as if the 'line' had gone dead. Was he ill? Was he hurt? Was he in danger? It was hard to tell.

'Hold on Chico. I'm coming to Rio tomorrow. I'll contact you when I get there. Stay safe.'

She hoped her messages were getting through to him. Still she wouldn't know until she arrived in Brazil.

Until then she could only pray.

CHAPTER TWENTY FIVE

Indigo found it difficult to sit still on the long flight to Rio. Since receiving the SOS call from Chico she had been feeling a mixture of anxiety and frustration but now she was sitting on the plane, next to Brandon, looking out of the small window at an aerial view of Rio de Janeiro at night. There was just no other word for it. It was breathtaking. The statue of Jesus stood on top of the Corcovado Mountain, lit up like the Christmas cross outside her village church, and keeping vigil over the many souls, who were darting about the city below her. She wondered where Chico would be amongst the many twinkling lights. She had tried to contact him on the plane but it had been hopeless.

'Wow,' exclaimed Brandon, leaning over her to get a better look, 'have you ever seen anything like that before.'

It wasn't really a question. They sat mesmerised at the view of the city below. A huge football stadium dominated the city, the green turf, lit by a bank of bright lights.

'Hey, look at that football stadium. It's huge. You know they love their soccer in Brazil. Any chance we can get to a game?' he asked Juliet.

She leant across Brandon to get a better view.

'I can check whether there is a game on while we're here. We've got two days in Rio before we head to the rainforest. But I don't know what the others' plans are so we'll have to see. Isn't it fabulous?'

The 'others' were a group of disadvantaged and challenging young people from London who were joining them on their trip to the rainforest. It was meant to be a character building exercise to help them learn life skills Juliet had told them. They were meeting up with them at the airport when they landed. Indigo hadn't given them much thought until just then. She had been too busy worrying about Chico.

I wonder what they'll be like.

The pilot announced their arrival at the airport and welcomed them all to Rio.

'Would that be the "Rio de Janeiro Galeao Antonio Carlos Jabim International Airport"?' Brandon asked Indigo, mocking her earlier delight of possibly the longest airport name in the world.

'I believe it is!' she replied with equal sarcasm, smiling back at him and beginning to feel very excited now they had finally landed after such a long flight.

Her thoughts turned to Chico.

Please be safe and well.

It seemed like an age before they had finished claiming their bags and going through passport control and now they had to wait for the others to join them from a later flight. The plan was to pick up a hired minibus and drive to the hotel where Indigo had decided she would flop into bed and sleep for a week.

'Here they are,' Juliet announced waving at them.

A throng of young people were emerging from customs control. They were with a very tall, black guy who a head full of dreadlocks tied into a thick clump at the back of his neck. They reached down to his waist. Juliet greeted him with a hug and a kiss to his cheek.

'This is Kash, the youth worker I told you about and I guess these are his group.'

Kash smiled, showing a row of shining white teeth. Indigo liked him. She sensed good vibes from this visually striking character. They were introduced to a dissolute bunch of kids who grunted and mostly kept their heads down, avoiding eye contact.

With the introductions over Kash went to pick up the minibus from the hire company.

Indigo whispered to Brandon that she was going to sit down and see if she could contact Chico. Now that she had set foot on Brazilian soil she thought she might have better luck. She moved a little way from the group to a set of bench chairs where she sat straight-backed with her hands on her lap; her palms turned upwards and closed her eyes. She took a deep breath and zoned out. One of the girls from the other group, who had been introduced as Letitia, noticed her and sidled over.

'What she doin?' she asked Brandon, pulling a face as if the act of asking the question pained her.

Brandon thought for a long time before answering her. 'She's trying to communicate …err…get in touch with…someone.'

'I know's what 'communicate' means,' she said, making speech marks with her hands. 'You think 'cos I is black that I is dumb?' Letitia jibed, mocking herself. 'Why don't she try her mobile phone?'

'Good question. But that would only work if the other party had a mobile phone.'

'The other party,' Letitia repeated, layered with heavy sarcasm, 'Hey, check this guy out.'

She turned to the other group who had gathered round all laughing and mimicking Brandon's accent. The noise disturbed Indigo. She opened her eyes and become aware for the first time of the others standing around her. The girl who had been introduced as Letitia appeared to be the ring leader.

She was dressed in a pair of skimpy denim shorts with a strappy T shirt that showed off her smooth, brown midriff. The most striking thing about her was the amount of gold jewellery she had around both her neck and her wrists. Indigo thought she looked like one of those beautiful gypsies in old movies, mysterious and fiery. She felt the hostile vibes, something she hadn't felt since the school bully, Georgina had tormented her. It brought back painful memories. She pushed them from her mind.

'Hi. What's going on? Why is everyone staring at me?'

Letitia took the lead. 'Manage to contact 'the other party?' she asked, her voice changing to cheerful sarcasm.

The bangles on her wrists jangled as she made speech marks in the air.

'Oh that. No. I haven't been able to. I'll try again later.'

She stood up, smiled at Letitia and took Brandon's arm. She could see Juliet heading their way and used it as a diversion.

'Here comes Juliet.'

Juliet was pushing through the crowds towards them, gesturing for them to follow her.

'Come on. Kash has picked up the minibus and is waiting for us outside. Follow me all of you and stay close.'

The group pushed past Indigo and Brandon to follow Juliet.

'Freak,' Letitia muttered to Indigo as she pushed past her.

'What did you say to them?' asked Indigo when she was clear of the group.

'Well, it was tricky. I thought about our pledge, you know, to not tell a living soul, but I could see she wasn't the kind of person who would believe me even if I told her the truth.' He smiled. 'So I decided to tell her the truth since I was pretty sure she wouldn't believe me anyway. Couldn't think of anything else to say,' he shrugged.

'Just exactly what did you say?'

Indigo was curious now. She didn't want any trouble but it looked like Letitia might be a handful.

'That you were communicating with another party.'

Indigo laughed.

'So that's where that came from!'

They all clambered into the mini-bus, stowing and securing their luggage on the roof racks above them. The journey to the hotel room passed off without incident. Everyone was tired and it was all they could do to keep awake. Indigo gazed out of the window at the colourful streets, the tall buildings and the crowds of people, hanging on street corners. Rio was buzzing with life even at this time of night.

Chico is out there somewhere. I must find him.

When they arrived at the hotel it was late. Juliet and Kash seemed keen to get everyone booked in and settled down for the night.

Indigo was shown into her room by a young boy who didn't seem much older than herself. He had carried her rucksack up to her room and having placed it on her bed was now standing there. Indigo wondered if she was expected to say or do something. She wasn't sure whether he was expecting a tip from her.

'Is everything all right?' he asked looking around the room.

'It's great, thank you.'

'Thank you, madam. Have a pleasant stay.'

The boy lingered for a while. Indigo wondered why he was still there. Then it clicked. He was waiting for a tip. She fumbled in her bag and took out her travel wallet. Rifling through the unfamiliar notes she hoped to find a low denomination to give him as a tip. The boy must have realised her dilemma because he turned to go and bid her goodnight.

'Oh,' I'm sorry...'

He smiled at her. 'No problem, madam. Enjoy your stay.'

'Oh, thank you. Goodnight.'

'That was an awkward moment and how embarrassing being called 'Madam' she laughed to herself after locking the door and flopping onto the bed. Her thoughts turned to Chico and of trying to contact him again but her body and mind told her she was just too tired.

CHAPTER TWENTY SIX

The storm began sometime after midnight. Indigo couldn't sleep. She lay on her back looking up at the mosquito net suspended above her. Unlike the one in her bedroom this had a very practical use. Mosquitoes, she had discovered, liked to take bites out of her. She lay there listening to an orchestra of baying hounds and barking dogs. They had been keeping her awake. Perhaps they felt it too. The shift in earthly vibrations. She watched as the flashes of lightening lit up her bedroom, illuminating shadows in the corners of her room, then counted the seconds to the next roll of thunder. It was getting closer and louder.

The rain began in splodges at first then as the thunder exploded outside her bedroom, it sounded like a thousand horses galloping on the roof above. In the tiled courtyard outside she could hear the wind whipping up the leaves and debris. As the strength of the wind gained, it loosened the wooden shutters from their fastening slamming them against the outside wall. The noise was tremendous. Another deafening crack of thunder ripped through the sky, this time it was followed by total blackness. The electricity supply had gone.

She tiptoed across to the window and looked out at the sprawling city. The bright lights of night-time Rio were no longer, extinguished like the light of a candle. She understood now why people spoke of the rumbling of thunder and the flashing of lightening. She'd never felt so close to the power of nature. Flash. Her room went from pitch black to white light, flashing on and off like a broken light bulb. The pitch blackness returned. She felt her way back to her bed, counting the seconds again, waiting for the next boom of thunder. As she lay there, she heard a faint tap on her door and a quiet voice whispering her name.

'Are you awake? Can I come in?'

It sounded like Letitia. Indigo unfurled her mosquito net, jumped out of bed and went to the door. When she opened it, she saw a wide-eyed and frightened little girl before her, not the wild gypsy from earlier. Stripped of her jewellery, she stood in her pyjamas, looking small and not intimidating at all. Right on cue, a thunderclap broke.

Letitia ran past Indigo, jumped on to the bed, wrapped her arms around her knees in a huddled position and asked if she could stay until the storm was over. Indigo smiled, closing the door behind her.

'Of course you can.'

Letitia's face softened.

'I figured you the kinda person who would deal with this kinda stuff well. No good goin' to the others. They bigger wusses than me when it comes to thunder and lightning.'

Indigo climbed in beside her and re-arranged the net.

'Good job it's a double bed.'

Letitia remained huddled.

'Are you going to sleep like that?' Indigo asked her, trying to inject some humour in to the situation to calm her down.

'Won't be able to sleep. Not with this going on.'

Letitia's voice sounded odd.

'Are you okay?' inquired Indigo.

Letitia was wheezing and taking short rapid breaths.

'I have 'azma',' she replied, in between shallow breaths, pronouncing asthma with a 'z'.

'Can I get you anything?'

'No, don't worry. I'll be okay in a minute. It'll pass.'

The sound of another thunder clap boomed overhead. Letitia clutched her thin legs tighter, burying her head into her bony knees.

Indigo's concern for Letitia grew as her breathing became quicker and more erratic.

Letitia spoke in between short breaths. 'I can't breathe. I need my inhaler.'

'Where is it? I'll go and get it.'

'In my bedroom.'

Indigo ran out and down the hallway, stopping outside Letitia's bedroom door. Once inside, she spotted her suitcase open on the floor. She rummaged around looking for the inhaler but found nothing. A quick scan around the room and into the bathroom. Still no inhaler. She rushed back to her room where she found Letitia lying on the bed, clutching at her chest unable to breathe.

No time to lose.

She placed both her hands on Letitia's chest, on her Heart Chakra. Letitia's frightened, black eyes were wide open and staring at the ceiling above. Her small face was framed by a mass of tight, black ringlets that had tumbled onto the white pillow case. Indigo closed her eyes and concentrated. She felt the familiar warm energy flow into her and then on into Letitia's lungs. By degrees, she felt Letitia's breathing ease. Her heartbeat slowed down until at last she was breathing normally. Indigo opened her eyes to see Letitia's eyes were open and she was smiling.

'How do you feel?'

'I feel good…really good.' She sat up, seeming to forget her fear of the storm and touched her chest. 'Wow. That was good. I felt heat coming from your hands into my chest. Right here. It's still warm. It was like the heat was goin' in my lungs. My chest don't feel tight anymore.' She breathed in through her nose, the nostrils flaring. 'See. That's the first time I can remember really filling my lungs full of air. That feels so good.'

It was hard to believe, looking and listening to Letitia that she was the hard bitten, street wise kid with attitude that had treated Indigo with such disrespect earlier in the day. Just a frightened little child deep inside hitting out at a world that hasn't treated her with the same respect.

That will change.

'What did you do, girl? You some kinda witch doctor? How did you do that?'

She fired question after question at Indigo wanting to know more.

'I just called upon the Universe's healing energy and channelled it into you.'

'You did what?'

The sarcasm from earlier was gone from her voice.

'It's a thing I seem to be able to do. Heal people.'

Indigo waited. In the short time she had known Letitia; she had felt intimidated by her.

How would she react now?

'We need to talk, girl. You gotta tell me all about this 'Universal Energy'.'

The temperature in the room had dropped a few degrees so they both snuggled under the covers. They talked long into the night, sharing stories about their lives and families. Letitia had been born in Sierra Leone and was brought over to London by her grandmother when she was ten, whilst her mother had stayed in Sierra Leone. Her father had abandoned her mother shortly after she was born so she didn't know him. Indigo, at last, felt she had something in common with her new friend. She didn't know who her father was either. Although it seemed like their lives were worlds apart Indigo felt a connection to Letitia, like specks of stardust from the same planet.

CHAPTER TWENTY SEVEN

Chico had decided to run away from Carlos. He had lived on the streets long enough to know that no-one could be trusted. If he was to come out of this alive he knew he had to find somewhere he could hide to buy him some time so he could think about how he was going to get out of the mess he was in.

Carlos knew a lot of people. Everyone feared him. There were lots of people who owed him favours; still more who would be happy to find Chico for him in return for a few Brazilian Real. He had decided to hide in an old building by the city's zoo that was boarded up and derelict. No-one would ever think of looking for him there. He knew it well. He used to hang around the zoo entrance hoping for an opportunity to sneak past the ticket collectors or beg money from the tourists to try to get enough to buy his own ticket. His dream was to see the animals inside but he had never managed to gain entry. Usually, he was sent away by the zoo staff and told not to come back.

One day, when he had been feeling weary after a day hanging around the zoo entrance, he decided to explore an old house close by. He had found a way in and spent the night. Since then, it had become his secret place.

He had been walking for a long time when a dark and fierce storm descended. The thunder and lightning didn't bother him, he had other troubles tonight, but he did think of the animals back at Carlos'. They would be frightened and he wasn't there to re-assure them. As he turned the corner, into the howling wind, the house stood tall and black against the night sky. He had begun to feel a little strange on the way there but had put that down to tiredness. Now the stomach ache he had put down to hunger was turning into severe cramps. His eyesight seemed to be affected. Nothing seemed straight and he stumbled into objects he couldn't see.

In the darkness, he felt around for the gap in the boarded up window. He tugged at the rotting boarding which gave way easily. It took all his strength to climb up and squeeze himself through the narrow gap. He felt dizzy and unsure on his feet. As he lowered himself into the vast hallway, he lost his grip and fell the last few feet. His strength and agility was ebbing away. It took all his remaining strength to climb the staircase to his secret room.

The building had once been a grand and elegant hotel. Crumbling plaster and holes in the ceilings, where the room above could be seen, added to the ghostly feel of the building in the thick blackness of the storm. He imagined the majestic balls and grandiose banquets attended by wealthy guests, the women in their beautiful gowns, the men wearing cummerbunds and bow ties. An eternity from the life he had lived. He had only seen such things in magazines.

He crawled up the grand staircase, hanging on to the rungs of the balustrade to pull him up. Some of the rungs were missing and what was left looked very precarious. After a great deal of effort, Chico found the old linen cupboard where he slept and closed the door behind him. A heap of old curtains lay on the floor where he had left them. He collapsed, utterly exhausted, on top of them.

He dreamt about his mother. She seemed very real to him. He was wrapped in her arms and he could smell her hair and feel the soft, warm touch of her skin. The dreamlike feeling of being safe, protected and loved came back to him but then he woke up and the intense sadness that followed, once he realised it was just a dream, overwhelmed him. His heart felt like it was breaking into small pieces, the physical pain, unbearable. He wiped away tears that were trickling down his hot cheek. His clothes were clinging to his body which felt damp and clammy, yet his skin felt as though it were burning. He could feel the blood pumping through his veins, thick and heavy, like the molten rays of a hot sun, thudding through his chest into his heart which was breaking. He tried to lift his head but it felt like a brick football. He tried to raise his hand to wipe the sweat from his face but that too was like a heavy log. He gave up trying.

What day is it? What time is it? How long have I been lying here? Where am I?

He looked around the room but found it difficult to focus. The walls seemed to be closing in on him. He closed his eyes and lost consciousness.

CHAPTER TWENTY EIGHT

Indigo woke the next morning to find Letitia still lying next to her in the bed, sleeping soundly. The sun was already finding its way through the cracks in the shutters, casting shards of yellow light on the dark floor tiles, heating up the room. She tried not to wake Letitia as she got out of bed. Early morning was a good time to connect on the grid, when there was less chatter and interference. She tiptoed across the room and sat in the corner.

In the stillness, she closed her eyes and tuned into the grid. It was very faint but she caught the sense of Chico's presence. She could sense his pain. Concentrating all of her powerful thoughts on him, she managed to get through to him, but the connection was fuzzy. She asked him where he was and whether he was well. All she could make out was the word 'zoo'. She asked again. The same word. 'Zoo'.

'What do you mean? Where are you?'

No answer. Nothing. She opened her eyes to find Letitia standing over her. She was scratching her head as if puzzling over something.

'You tuning in to that Universal Energy again, girl. What is it wit' you?'

She wandered out of the room without waiting for an answer still talking to herself.

'Gotta get some breakfast. I could eat a whole pig I feel so good.'

Indigo was grateful for the fact that Letitia was still half asleep so she didn't have to explain anything or worse still, lie. She got dressed and went downstairs for breakfast, seeking out Brandon, who was already sitting at a table finishing his breakfast.

'You're late. I knocked on your door but got no answer. You okay? You look tired.'

'Bit of a heavy night with Letitia.'

'Oh no! What has she done to you?'

'Not what you're thinking,' she began.

'Phew, got me worried for a second there.'

'We haven't been fighting or anything like that. She was afraid of the storm and slept in my room.'

'Yeah, the storm. Didn't hear a thing. Slept right through it.'

Typical Brandon.

'I've managed to contact Chico.'

'You have? Is he okay?'

'I can't be certain but I think he's in trouble. I couldn't get a good enough connection. He seemed distant somehow.'

She poured some juice into a glass and buttered a bread roll.

'So what are we going to do?'

'I kept hearing the word…zoo. What do you think that means?'

Brandon's brow furrowed as if in deep concentration. After a while he spoke.

'Maybe there's a zoo in Rio? Maybe he's at the zoo?'

'Of course. That's it. Brandon, you're a genius.'

They slapped each other's palms in a high five gesture, then carried on eating their breakfast. Letitia walked in with the rest of her gang and made her way towards them.

One of the girls shouted across, 'Hey look it's the freak from yesterday.' Letitia pushed her hard, almost knocking her into one of the tables where an elderly couple sat sipping tea. Indigo mouthed a silent 'sorry' to them in the absence of any apology from Letitia.

'Don't you diss Indigo,' she said to the girl. 'She ain't no freak, she for real.'

The girl looked confused as she made her way over to a table on the far side of the dining room. The others joined her where they sat looking dejected. Letitia walked over to Indigo and sat down.

'You won't get no more trouble from them. I'll make sure of that.'

Brandon looked like he'd seen a ghost.

'You feeling okay?' Letitia asked him.

Brandon snapped out of his shock.

'Sure. Never better.'

An uneasy silence fell between them.

'So what's going on?'

They both looked at her as if they weren't sure what she was talking about.

'Come on. You don't fool me. I can tell you two are up to something. Spill...'

She laid out both hands on the table, her pink palms turned upwards. She waited. The uneasy silence re-surfaced like an unwelcome guest.

'I don't know what you mean...' began Brandon.

'It's okay Brandon,' Indigo interrupted, 'I think Letitia might be able to help us.'

'What makes you think that?' he questioned, looking hurt, a hint of jealousy creeping in.

'We were just wondering if there was a zoo in Rio.'

Letitia raised her eyebrows.

'Do you know if there is one?' Indigo asked her, not giving anything away.

'There's only one way to find out,' she replied.

She grabbed a hand full of bread rolls, stood up and, taking hold of Indigo's hand, dragged her out of the breakfast room.

Letitia looked behind her to find a wide - mouthed Brandon still sitting at the table.

'You comin' or you just gonna sit there and gawp all day?' Letitia shouted back at him.

Brandon shot up from the table as if he'd just been stung by a bee and followed them.

Out in the busy street, Letitia hailed a cab by shouting 'yo' to a passing taxi, which impressed Indigo. The taxi stopped and she asked, in near perfect English for the driver to take them to the zoo.

'*No problemo*,' the taxi driver said, showing his yellowed teeth. They all piled into the back of the car and the taxi moved off into the busy traffic of Rio.

Letitia took out some lip gloss from her handbag and applied it to her lips without the need for a mirror.

'Well that was easy. Looks like there is a zoo in Rio. What you want to go there for anyhows?'

'We like animals…' Brandon told her.

Silence.

'We love animals…' Indigo offered.

She put the lip gloss back in her handbag and snapped it shut.

'Why do I get the feeling this ain't just about a trip to the zoo because you both like animals? This is Lerr-titia you talking to. I sense action. I sense adventure. You two running away from home?'

Brandon couldn't help himself and he burst out laughing.

'I don't recall saying anything funny?' she glared at him.

'Sorry,' he said, coming to his senses, 'it's just you couldn't be further from the truth.'

'Some truth would be good just now...'

Indigo sat between them, feeling like piggy in the middle. She had been thinking about whether it was a good idea or not to just tell Letitia the real reason they were going to the zoo. Sometimes telling the truth was the best course of action in certain situations. Was this one of those times, she pondered. Letitia was no fool. She would find out sooner or later and besides she seemed to be pretty resourceful. She decided to take a chance.

'We're looking for someone.'

'Who might that be?'

'A boy. We think he might be in trouble.'

'What kinda trouble?'

'We don't know yet but we have to find him.'

'And you think you gonna find him at the zoo? Why the zoo? What has this boy got to do with the zoo?' she fired back.

'We don't know that either, yet,' Indigo answered.

'So, we going on a wild goose chase for some boy who may be in trouble and may be at the zoo?'

'Yeah, that's about it,' Brandon concluded, crossing his arms and looking out at the streets of Rio.

'Bring it on!' Letitia raised her hand, 'High five!'

'High five!' Indigo returned the gesture, slapping her hand against the hand of her new friend.

'You too,' Letitia invited, raising her hand towards Brandon.

Indigo dug him in the side. He turned round, and scowled at her and then he saw Letitia smiling at him with her arm raised. He relented, smiled back and raised his hand to give Letitia the loudest 'high five' he could manage.

Thwack.

CHAPTER TWENTY NINE

The taxi moved through the traffic logged streets of Rio at the pace of a snail. They sat in the back listening to the air conditioning blasting out of the vents and drowning out the radio which sounded like Salsa music played by a brass band. Letitia leaned forward and spoke to the driver.

'Any chance of some decent music?'

'You no like my music?' he answered her in English but with a thick Hispanic accent, gesticulating with his left hand while looking in his mirror at Letitia. He appeared hurt by the slur of his choice of music. Indigo wished that Letitia could just sit quietly and mind her own business.

'Don't distract him. He's driving,' she said, hoping Letitia would take the hint but Letitia was like an embarrassing member of the family who always turned up at family events and who you couldn't escape from.

'You in Latin America now. You have to listen to Salsa? No?' the driver continued.

'Yeah, but not by a brass band.'

Indigo decided to change the subject and asked the driver how much farther it was. She had visions of being thrown out in the middle of a city she was not familiar with, getting lost and possibly, even worse, being mugged. The

171

taxi pulled up outside the zoo's impressive arched entrance. The arch led into an avenue of tall Royal palms which cast a welcome shade. Letitia jumped out of the taxi and wandered over to the arch, leaving them to pay the taxi fare.

'She's a nightmare, Indigo. What on earth were you thinking, getting her involved?'

'I didn't really. She sort of got herself involved. Anyway, I think she may be really useful. She got us here didn't she?'

'Yeah, at our expense,' he sulked as he handed over his share of the fare.

'*Obrigado.*'

Indigo thanked the driver in Portuguese. He smiled at her, flashing his tobacco stained teeth.

'*Obrigado, Senhorita. Adeus.*'

Indigo turned to walk away but Brandon held her arm to stop her.

'Are you going to tell her everything?'

'Not sure yet. I might have to.'

'Do you trust her?'

They both looked over at Letitia who was standing under the arch, hands on hips, waiting for them.

'I think we might have to.'

'We?' he protested.

'Yes "we". We're in this together aren't we?' she raised her eyebrows and looked at Brandon with an enquiring look.

He opened his mouth to say something, and then closed it again. 'I guess so,' he mumbled, thrusting his hands into his pockets.

'Come on then.'

She took hold of his arm and dragged him toward impatient Letitia. A few people were milling up and down the avenue, mostly with small children in tow. Indigo chose a cool, quiet spot out of the nailing heat of the sun. She had to concentrate. If Chico was anywhere nearby, she felt sure she could find him.

'So where is your friend? He in the zoo?'

'We don't know where he is yet,' Indigo answered her.

'You said earlier he was in some kinda trouble? Perhaps he wandered into the lion enclosure?' she joked. 'He in that kinda trouble? Or is it something else?'

Indigo could tell she wanted to know more, that she wasn't going to stop asking questions until she was satisfied she'd got all the right answers.

'Can you give me a few minutes, Letitia?'

'Sure.'

'Hopefully, I'll be able to answer all your questions. I just don't have all the answers myself, yet.'

Indigo leant against the carved stone arch and pressed her bony spine against the solid coolness. She closed her eyes.

'She gonna do that thing again like she did at the airport?' Letitia asked.

Brandon pulled on her arm. 'Just give her some space.' He led her down the avenue towards the zoo's entrance gates. 'I think I need to explain a few things,' he began.

He told her all about the pet shop, how they had stumbled across an illegal pet smuggling ring and how they had been invited to come to Brazil to re-home the monkey. Letitia listened without interrupting him. He told her about Chico contacting Indigo in England before they left and that he had said he was in trouble and asked Indigo to help him.

When he had finished, she asked in a quiet, thoughtful voice.

'Is Indigo psychic?'

'I think I better let Indigo explain that bit.'

They heard footsteps running towards them from behind. It was Indigo and she was looking very pleased with herself.

'He's here. I've found him but we have to be quick. Something's definitely wrong.'

Letitia was staring at Indigo. 'You a strange girl. You really psychic?'

'Kind of. But I don't have time to explain that now. Come on.'

She turned back towards the arch and started running.

'He said to find the old building by the zoo. The one that looks like it's falling down.'

They scanned the road, left to right.

'It's this way,' Indigo yelled.

They marched along the perimeter of the zoo enclosure until they came to a corner at a road junction. Again they scanned the road.

'Is that it?' Brandon pointed to an old building set back from the road. The plaster was flaking and grey and the gated entrance looked rusted and unused. Indigo didn't answer. She ran on towards the gates. They were locked.

'Let's try round the back,' suggested Brandon.

Brandon took the lead, followed by Indigo and then Letitia who trailed behind, hobbled by her fashion shoes. The stone wall changed into a wooden fence which they traced until they found a broken panel. Brandon gave it a few kicks, it gave way easily. The dried out wood was brittle and cracked with a loud snap which echoed through the trees. He popped his head through the fence and looked from side to side to check no-one was there, and then slipped through the gap turning to help the girls get through the fence before heading off again.

The gardens had once been very grand but sadly they had been neglected and were overgrown. They made their way past stone statues, with weathered faces, peeking from strangler figs. An ornamental pond, long since emptied of cool water, stood in the grounds, its base cracked concrete and weeds. Indigo stopped and sat on the low wall.

'I just need a few minutes to concentrate,' she said, brushing hair from her face.

Letitia sat down, kicking off her shoes. She stretched out her lean, brown legs and wiggled her purple-painted toenails. Brandon carried on up the stone steps that led to the house. At the top he looked back.

Indigo was sat, straight backed with her palms upturned and her eyes closed. He sat on the steps and took out his handkerchief. Wiping the back of his neck and face, he waited. Indigo came running up the steps.

'He's definitely here. He's inside the house.'

They waited for Letitia who was tip-toeing up the steps making 'ouch' noises as her bare feet stepped onto sharp bits of gravel.

'Why don't you put your shoes back on?' Brandon asked, sighing out of impatience.

'They don't wanna go on any more. My feet have swelled up.'

Brandon didn't bother to answer, just raised his eyebrows and carried on towards the house. Ahead of him, Indigo had found the broken window board and was climbing in. By the time the others had reached her she was inside and running up the staircase.

'Careful,' shouted Brandon, 'they don't look safe.'

Indigo appeared not to hear. She reached the landing and disappeared out of sight. Brandon rushed after her, leaving Letitia to deal with the unsafe stairs in her own way. Indigo opened the door to the linen room and found Chico lying on the floor covered in the old curtains. She ran across to him and knelt down. She pulled the curtains back to reveal Chico's tiny body, lying motionless. He looked like he was asleep.

'Chico,' she whispered.

No response.

'Is he dead?' she heard Letitia ask from close behind her.

'I don't know. I can't tell.'

The three of them stood over Chico looking at his lifeless body.

'Here,' said Letitia, taking out a small makeup mirror from her bag and handing it to her, 'Put this to his mouth. If it fogs up, he's alive.'

'Are you sure about this?'

'I sin it on TV. Go on, try it.'

Indigo held the mirror to Chico's dry, cracked lips. They waited. She pulled back the mirror and there on the surface was the tell-tale signs of fogging.

'He's alive,' she breathed.

Letitia made a whooping sound, which in the circumstances they were in seemed wholly inappropriate.

'Shush...' hissed Brandon.

Indigo touched Chico's forehead. She hadn't dared to before, fearing he might be dead. It was on fire. She rummaged in her rucksack and took out a bottle of water and some tissues. She wet the tissue and swabbed his forehead and cheeks, then trickled some water onto his dry lips. He moaned and his eyelids fluttered, only the whites of his eyes showing. He had taken on a ghoulish appearance. Undeterred, she placed her hands on his stomach and closed her eyes. After only a few moments, she opened her eyes and a terrified expression fell across her face.

'We need to get him to a hospital, now. If we don't, he's going to die.'

The word 'die' hung in the air between them reminding them how perilous the situation was.

'Can't you do your thing?' Letitia asked, urgency in her voice.

'It's not working. Something is blocking the energy.'

Indigo was close to tears. Brandon took over. He pushed Indigo out of the way, scooped Chico's limp body into his arms and made his way to the door.

'Indigo, run on ahead and see if you can call a taxi. We'll follow you.'

He knew it was no use asking Letitia given her foot problems. Indigo flew down the stairs, through the garden and found her way back to the road.

She couldn't keep still, pacing up and down the road, looking for a taxi and praying to the Universe for a taxi to show up. She didn't have to wait long. She waved her arms around like a mad thing to attract the taxi-driver's attention. Without looking, she stepped into the road in front of an oncoming car. The taxi's brakes screeched sending dust into the air and into Indigo's eyes. She slapped her hands on the bonnet of the car, relieved that it had managed to stop in time, and then ran round to the driver's side. He was shouting and cursing and gesticulating all in Portuguese. Indigo caught the word 'Madonna' but took no notice of him.

'This is an emergency. I have a sick friend and you must take us to the hospital.'

The driver stopped in mid curse and gave her a blank look.

'SOS,' she shouted into his face. 'Hospital. Amigos.'

She pointed towards Brandon who was by now struggling to carry Chico. She dug in her jeans' pocket and pulled out some Brazilian notes. The driver cursed again, but then he saw the money.

'*Hopital?*' he asked, changing his expression to one of undisguised greed.

'Si, Si, Pronto,' replied Indigo, not sure what language she was talking in.

He seemed to understand in any case. He started the engine and jabbed this thumb backwards indicating to them to get in the back. They squeezed in, lying Chico across their laps. His body felt burning hot and clammy at the same time. Beads of perspiration covered his forehead and top lip. His skin looked pallid and grey. The driver performed a dramatic U-turn in the road and carried on, weaving his way through the traffic-swamped streets. Indigo, sitting in the middle, searched out the hands of Brandon and Letitia and squeezed them hard. She felt a strong squeeze back.

All will be well. All will be well.

Brandon asked Indigo for the water bottle, took out his handkerchief, soaked it and then placed it across Chico's forehead. The back of the taxi remained silent. Then panic set in. Chico started to convulse. His tiny frame twitched and snapped. His teeth were clenched into a grimace and white foam was oozing from his mouth.

'I think he's fitting,' cried Brandon, his voice tremulous with rising panic.

'Quick,' shouted Indigo. 'Turn him over on his side or he'll swallow his tongue and choke.'

They struggled to turn him towards them. Indigo snatched the handkerchief, rolled it into a sausage shape and prised open Chico's mouth. She placed the cloth over his tongue, securing it to the bottom of his mouth, pushed his chin up to clamp his teeth together, and forced him to bite down on the cloth. The white foam continued to ooze from the corner of his mouth onto Brandon's jeans.

'*Qual é o problema?*' demanded the driver.

Letitia could only make out the word "problem" but quick thinking, she replied, 'No problem. He's epe...epepleptic,' pronouncing the word wrong. It didn't matter anyway. The driver kept on cursing and gesticulating.

After a few minutes, Chico lay still. Very still. Brandon asked for the mirror again. He placed it against Chico's clenched mouth. The fog appeared. He sunk back into his seat and gave a loud sigh. He was still alive.

CHAPTER THIRTY

'Damn that boy. When I find him, he'll wish he'd never been born,' cursed Carlos.

He was in the worst rage ever. He thrashed around the room, kicking boxes over, smashing his fists into animal cages and cursing everything in sight. The monkeys were screeching and trying to hide at the back of their small cages, eyes wide and frightened. The macaws were flapping their wings, hopping from branch to floor and back again, making a terrible, ear piercing squawk, desperate to escape from their prison.

Domingo and Juan sat very still and quiet, waiting for Carlos to stop. They sat in the dimness of the room, not daring to speak. They knew they were in for more trouble than they had ever known. Carlos turned on them.

'And what are you two doing sitting there like a pair of stuffed dummies? Get out there and find him. I want that boy back here and I want him now,' he bellowed at them.

The men rose to leave.

'And don't come back until you find him. Don't even think about coming back without him. I made you responsible for the boy and now he's disappeared. You know what will happen to you if you don't find him so I suggest you get out there and find him quick.'

Carlos slumped into a chair and took out a cigarette. He poured himself a large glass of Aguardente and slugged it down in one. He placed the unlit cigarette in his mouth and looked up at the two men. He took the cigarette back out of his mouth and spoke through clenched teeth.

'Are you two still here?'

Juan nudged Domingo.

'No, boss, we're outta here. No worries, we'll find the boy. You see, we do the job right this time. No worries.'

Juan patted his gun.

'Get out of my sight,' Carlos shouted.

He picked up his glass and threw it at Juan. Juan dodged the glass and was gone, leaving Carlos alone in a room full of frightened, noisy animals. He looked around him and thought about the boy. Although it pained him to acknowledge, he realised he had made a huge mistake. The boy was good with the animals, he had a gift. He should never have involved him in his new business venture. That was a mistake, but it was done and there was no way of going back. He picked up the bottle and took a swig.

Regret, for Carlos, was a sign of weakness. He pushed the feelings to the back of his mind. If he was to become rich and powerful in the favela he could not show weakness of any kind. He felt the familiar burning sensation as the Aguardente slipped down his throat and into his stomach, burning away any weakness with it.

CHAPTER THIRTY ONE

The taxi pulled up outside the hospital. Letitia opened her door and slid her legs from underneath Chico's. Brandon pushed Chico's frail body towards her, then jumped out the other side and ran round to catch hold of him. He picked him up and ran into the emergency department, leaving Indigo to pay the disgruntled taxi driver.

By the time she walked into the reception area, Chico had already been placed on a trolley. A doctor was leaning over him with a stethoscope, listening to his heart. He unbuttoned Chico's grubby shirt, shouting orders. A machine was wheeled toward them. She had seen a machine like this before and knew what it was going to be used for.

Chico's heart had stopped. Her own heart felt like it had been clamped it felt so tight. She watched the frantic scene unfold before her. The doctor took hold of the pads which were attached to the machine by curly plastic wires and placed them onto Chico's chest. He shouted something and everyone took a few steps back.

'*Pois bem!*' he commanded.

A nurse pressed a switch on the machine. There was a soft, whirring sound which built to a loud buzzing. She saw Chico's limp body jerk upwards as the electric current entered his heart. Everyone watched the monitor on the machine. No sound.

'*Repetir!*'

Again whirring, buzzing, more jerking of Chico's lifeless body. Everyone stared at the silent monitor.

'*Uma mais vez!*'

One more time.

Chico's body jerked again. A moment passed, and then the machine came to life, beeping and flashing. Squiggly green lines appeared on the screen. Indigo dropped to the floor, sobbing with relief. Brandon came over to her, put his arm around her and helped her to her feet. She looked up to see Chico being wheeled into an operating theatre at the end of the corridor. Burying her head into Brandon's shoulder, she clung to him. Letitia offered her a tissue. She managed a weak smile of thanks and gave her nose a good blow. Letitia, she noticed, was also blowing her nose, a sign that she had been crying. They sat down on a bench, the girls sniffing and blowing their noses. The only calm person was Brandon but he looked tired and sullen.

Various people walked past them whilst they sat and waited for news of their friend. Doctors carrying clipboards, porters wheeling patients, others lying down on trolleys. Some patients were screaming from their injuries, others looked in shock. Every now and then Indigo and her friends would glance towards the theatre door but no-one had gone in or come out. Not much was said between them apart from futile questions that neither of them knew the answer to but felt compelled to ask of one another.

'Do you think he's all right?'

'What do you think they're doing in there?'

'How long are they going to be?'

The ceiling fans whirred above them giving some respite from the heat and the harsh smell of disinfectant. The theatre door opened and as if trained to do it they all jumped up off the bench. It was the same doctor. He walked towards them, holding a clipboard and looking very tired. Indigo noticed he had dark circles under his eyes and his shoulder length hair was greasy. He spoke to them in Portuguese which they didn't understand. Then Indigo asked, in English, if Chico was all right.

'Ah, you are English. I am Doctor Mendez.'

He spoke English with an American accent.

'Is he all right?' she asked again.

'Your friend is very ill…but he will live.'

Indigo looked up at the ceiling and gave a silent 'thank you' to the Universe.

'Is this boy a friend of yours?' he asked.

'Yes…Well sort of. We only met him today,' she answered.

'Where did you meet him?'

Indigo hesitated. She didn't want to tell the doctor that they had broken into someone's property. He would want to know how she knew he was there. Letitia rescued her.

'We found him on the street. He looked really ill so we brought him here.'

The doctor looked like he wasn't sure whether to believe them or not.

'Well, there's no doubt you've saved his life.'

'What's the matter with him?' asked Indigo.

'Your friend is suffering from opioid intoxication.'

Blank faces stared back at him.

'He has swallowed large amounts of cocaine.'

Indigo gasped and her hand went to her mouth. 'Cocaine?' she repeated.

The doctor nodded. He looked at them all in turn, rubbing his unshaven chin. He continued to quiz them. 'Do you know anything about this?'

'Nothing. Absolutely nothing. We just thought he was ill.'

Indigo felt her lip curling and the tears welling up again.

'You really had no idea about this and you don't know who this boy is?'

'No. None.'

'I believe you,' he said, patting her shoulder. 'You've all done very well today. If it were not for your swift actions this boy would be dead now.'

Indigo wiped a tear from the corner of her eye with the back of her hand.

'Excuse me, Doctor Mendez. What's going to happen to him now?' Brandon asked.

'Well, body packing is a serious business. The police will want to interview him.'

More blank faces.

'Body packing?'

Doctor Mendez shook his head.

'You really have no idea what you've got yourselves involved in, have you?' he said, sounding concerned. 'Come on. Let's go get a cold drink. I think I need to explain a few things. You look like you could do with some refreshment and I know I certainly could.'

They sat round a table in the busy hospital café while the doctor brought over some ice cold bottles of Coke. Brandon put his bottle to his forehead to cool down before taking large gulps.

Doctor Mendez explained. 'The boy is what you call a drug mule.'

Letitia gave a look of recognition.

'You know what this is?' he questioned.

She nodded. 'It's what they call people who hide drugs inside their bodies, innit?'

'That's right.'

They all looked at her as if to say 'how does she know that?'

'I sin it on TV, that's all,' she defended herself.

'Someone has given this boy a large amount of cocaine to smuggle out of the country, possibly across the border to Paraguay. They pack the drug into small plastic packages. The drug mule swallows the packages and then takes something to make them constipated so they don't pass the packages naturally before they get to their destination. Once inside the body they can't be detected easily. Then when they get where they're going they take laxatives or enemas to expel their cargo.'

Letitia squirmed. 'Ugh. Too much information.'

Doctor Mendez continued. 'Your boy wasn't so lucky. Whoever gave him the drugs didn't pack it properly. They didn't use a second wrapper. One of the packets had ruptured – split open – inside him causing the effects of opioid intoxication.'

'Like a drug overdose?' Brandon asked.

'Exactly.'

Indigo couldn't help seeing images of Chico lying helpless and she shuddered as she realised just how close he had been to dying.

She also understood why her healing powers hadn't worked. They were useless against the powerful effects of such a drug.

'But why would anyone want to give a child drugs to smuggle out of the country?'

'The drug barons have started to use children because no one expects children to have cocaine on them. The authorities are less likely to suspect a child and more likely to suspect an adult. We see this sort of thing a lot these days. It's as simple as that.'

'But that's awful,' said Indigo, thinking of Chico sleeping on the streets.

'It's the life these street children live. You can't compare it to your own lives. These kids literally live on the street. They have no home, no parents. They don't go to school like you do and so they just do what they have to do to survive and I'm afraid in this city it's often drug dealing or stealing or getting involved in gangs.'

Indigo asked if he was going to get better.

'We had to carry out emergency surgery to remove the packages. 64 in total.'

Indigo shuddered, letting out a gasp.

'We followed with an aggressive gastro-intestinal decontamination and a naxolone infusion...'

'Whoa,' said Brandon, 'you're losing me.'

'Sorry. I forget who I'm speaking to sometimes.'

'But is he going to be okay?' Indigo repeated her question.

'He's stable now and sleeping. I've dealt with plenty of cases like these and in almost all cases the patient recovers with no long term damage.'

'What's going to happen to him?' asked Brandon.

'We'll fix him up and then hand him over to the police. He'll probably end up in jail like they all do.'

He rubbed his face in an attempt to wake himself up. It had been a long day.

'Such a waste of human life.' He stood up to leave. 'I have to go now.'

'Will the police want to speak to us?'

Doctor Mendez gave Indigo that questioning look as if he was reconsidering their innocence.

'I wouldn't think so. You found him on the street, didn't you?'

'Well…yes. I was just wondering that's all.'

She wanted to ask if she could see him but she thought better of it. She had already drawn suspicion. He would wonder why she wanted to see some boy she had just picked up off the street and didn't know. The doctor patted her hand.

'Don't worry about him. He's a street boy. That's the way they live. He knew what he was doing. At the end of the day it's all about survival for kids like that. Just forget about him and enjoy the rest of your holiday. I really have to go now.'

They thanked him for his time and said goodbye. As soon as he was out of earshot Letitia spoke.

'I never would have believed it looking at you two. Who would have thought you were mixed up in drug smuggling? And I thought you two were squeaky clean, a bit weird, but straight. Is that your cover – this monkey business?'

Whether it was out of nervous tension or the sheer absurdity that they would have anything to do with drugs, Indigo and Brandon turned to each other and collapsed into rib cracking laughter. Letitia failed to see what was so funny.

'When you're finished,' she began, 'perhaps you can start telling me what's going on here and I want the truth this time.'

Indigo held her stomach and tried to stop laughing but every time she looked at Brandon a fresh wave of hysteria rose up and took hold.

'I'm sorry. We weren't laughing at you.'

She took some deep breaths in an effort to calm herself down.

'Perhaps you can start by telling me how you knew that boy would be where we found him? And was all that eyes closed stuff an act to fool me?'

'Oh that.'

'Yes, that.'

'Okay. Let's see, where should I start?'

She took a deep breath and began her story. Now and then, Letitia would ask the odd question as if to catch her out. After several minutes of explanations Letitia seemed at last satisfied. Her butterfly mind had moved on.

'So, what you gonna do 'bout the boy?'

'What do you mean?' Indigo asked, startled.

'Well, he's a friend of yours, ain't he?'

'Yes, but…'

'Well, the way I see it, is this. That doctor took out 64 packets of cocaine from that boy's insides. That's a lotta cocaine.' She shook her hand, making a clacking noise with her fingers. 'Whoever gave him that will 'A', want to find the boy and 'B', want their drugs back and as he hasn't got the drugs on him anymore they're not going to be best pleased.'

'I hadn't thought about it that way. What do you think they'll do to him?'

'Kill him,' she said, with no trace of emotion.

Indigo's mouth fell open. She needed a few moments to take it all in. It all seemed so overwhelming, so unreal. Something was troubling her about the whole situation but she couldn't put her finger on it.

'I just need to speak to him before we go,' she announced.

She had her suspicions about who had given him the drugs but she wanted to know firsthand from Chico. A strong inner instinct told her it was important to find out more.

'Don't you think we're already way over our heads in this?' Brandon asked, running his hands through his messy hair.

'Probably, but I just need five minutes with him, then we can go.'

Brandon saw the pleading expression on Indigo's face and gave in.

CHAPTER THIRTY TWO

Juan and Domingo knew that if they didn't find the boy quickly, Carlos would become a very dangerous man to be around. They knew that the drugs had been given to Carlos by someone higher up in the drug world and that if he didn't get the drugs back, his life would be in danger. Juan knew that this time his own life was in danger. The stakes had been raised. Finding the boy was the only way out of this mess. They started by asking around the streets of Rio. Their first stop was Candelaria Church, the scene of the famous Candelaria Massacre where eight street children had been shot and killed by police on the steps of the church in a misguided effort to clean up the streets. It was still a popular hangout for street children. Street children were everywhere in Rio and it wasn't long before they found who they were looking for.

'Hey, Pedro,' they shouted at a small boy. 'You want to earn yourself a few Real?'

Within seconds they were thronged by a group of grubby street boys all clamouring to be given the few Real that was on offer. Juan knew that most of them hung around with Chico.

'Has anyone seen our little friend Chico?'

'What you want him for?' Pedro asked.

'No particular reason. We just haven't seen him for a few days that's all.'

'What's in it for me if I tell you?'

'Fifty Real if you tell us where to find him.'

There was a unified intake of breath from the boys followed by a chorus of shouts about knowing where to find Chico. Juan was conscious they were making a scene and that passersby were watching them. He didn't want to attract the attention of the local police. They grabbed hold of Pedro and pulled him away from the group, heading for an alleyway at the side of the church. The boys ran after them, chanting 'we know where he is, give us the money'. Juan turned on them and threatened to set the military police on to them – the very same police who had carried out the killings of the street children. The threat was enough and they ran off, leaving Pedro in the clutches of Juan and Domingo.

'Come on, don't waste our time. We know you know where he is. Tell us before Domingo here loses his temper. Pedro looked up at Domingo who sneered back at the boy, patting his gun holster under his t-shirt.

'I don't know where he is. I haven't seen him since yesterday.'

'Where did you see him?'

Pedro tried to wriggle out of Juan's grip. Domingo took hold of him and gripped his arm, twisting it behind his back. Pedro winced at the pain.

'I told you, I don't know nothing,' Pedro said, wincing.

'Not good enough. Try again.'

Juan nodded at Domingo. Domingo twisted tighter. Pedro cried out this time, the pain becoming unbearable.

'Okay, okay. I'll tell you what I know.'

Domingo released his grip on the young boy.

'I saw him yesterday evening. He was walking along Avenida Beira. He looked pretty bad to me.'

'What do you mean?' Juan demanded.

'He was walking pretty badly, stooped over and holding his stomach, like he had real bad gut ache. I didn't speak to him. It was raining real heavy and I was sleeping in the doorway of the Hotel Pereque trying to keep dry.'

'What time was that?'

'Around midnight, I guess.'

'And you haven't seen him since?'

'No. Not since then.'

Pedro made the sign of the cross.

'I promise. In the name of the Madonna and all that is holy.'

'Let him go.' Juan told Domingo. Domingo pushed the boy to the ground and walked off.

'Hey,' shouted Pedro after them, 'where is my fifty Real?'

They ignored the boy and carried on walking. They decided to stop off at a small bar on the way back to the car where they ordered two glasses of ice cold beer.

'What we gonna do now?' asked Domingo, pouring his beer down him until it gushed out the side of his wide mouth.

He wiped it away from his unshaven chin with his huge gorilla hands and took another mouthful. Juan studied the bubbles in his glass. He was thinking about what Carlos would do to them both if they didn't find the boy.

'The boy said he was unwell. Said he was holding his stomach. Maybe those bags he swallowed burst open. Maybe that's why he wasn't feeling so good.'

Domingo laughed out loud and slammed his drained beer glass onto the bar. Juan shot up out of his seat.

'You're a genius, Domingo. Come on.'

The slow-witted Domingo looked surprised. Juan emptied his glass of beer and jumped off the bar stool.

'Let's go check the hospital.'

CHAPTER THIRTY THREE

The children left the cafe and made their way back to the operating theatre, keeping a constant look out for Dr Mendez. The last thing they wanted was to bump into him and start all the questioning again. Indigo was like a hunting dog on the smell trail of a fox. She dashed off down a corridor, up some emergency stairs, down another corridor until she came to a door with a glass window.

'He's in there,' she whispered to her fellow hunters.

Letitia pushed open the door and walked in ahead of the others. The room was like a long corridor with at least a dozen beds, all occupied. Indigo followed scanning the room looking Chico. She ran towards a sleeping boy she thought looked like him.

'Here's here,' she beckoned them both over.

Letitia turned to Brandon and gushed. 'That girl is psychic to the max!'

'No doubt about that,' he replied.

Chico appeared to be asleep but when Indigo called his name, he opened his eyes.

'Hi Chico, it's Indigo.' She stroked his head.

'How are you feeling?'

Chico focused his eyes.

'Much better now, thank you.'

'I don't have much time Chico, the hospital staff might come back at any minute. I just wanted to ask who gave you the drugs.'

His eyes went blank and he turned away from her.

'Was it Carlos?' she asked, placing her hand around his bony little fingers.

Without looking back, he nodded.

'I thought so. But why did you do it? Did he make you?'

Chico turned to her and she could see tears in his eyes. He looked so small and innocent Indigo's heart ached at his sadness.

'He threatened to kill my mother if I didn't do it. I had no choice.'

'It's okay,' she re-assured him, squeezing his hand.

'What's going to happen to you now? Are you in a lot of trouble?'

'He will find me and kill me,' Chico croaked.

'Here, have some water.'

She put the glass to his dry lips.

'Thank you,' he croaked, sinking back onto the pillow.

'I know you're feeling weak Chico.'

She peeled off the covers and moved his legs over the side of the bed.

'But we need to get you out of here.'

'What are you doing?' hissed Brandon.

'I'm not leaving him here. It's not safe.'

'But where are you going to take him?' rising panic sounding in his voice.

Indigo already had Chico on his feet.

'Does anyone know about the house we found you in Chico?'

'No. I don't think so,' he replied, looking bewildered.

'We'll take him back there until we can sort something out. At least he will be safe there.'

Brandon pointed to Chico who was stood wearing only his underpants. 'You can't take him anywhere like that.'

'Hang on then.' Letitia walked over to the empty nurses' office. She checked the back of the door and re-emerged with a doctor's white coat. 'Take off your T-shirt and put this on.'

She threw the coat at Brandon. He whipped off his shirt and gave it to Indigo who pushed it over Chico's head. The shirt was far too big for him. It covered his knees. He looked comical, his thin, bony legs sticking out from under the shirt but it would have to do.

'Let's hope this works,' Brandon said.

Looking like a very junior doctor in his white coat Brandon led the way.

With Chico supported on both sides, they walked out of the hospital, unchallenged. They were so busy trying to keep Chico upright so as not to draw attention to themselves that they didn't notice the two grubby men watching them from the corner of the reception desk.

CHAPTER THIRTY FOUR

The only place Indigo could think to take Chico was back to the old house they had found him in. They took another taxi, stopping off at a shop to buy food and some water for him. He was still very weak and spent the journey asleep slumped against Brandon. When the taxi stopped, he woke.

'Where am I?' he breathed.

'You're back at the big house. You're sure no-one else knows about this house?' Indigo asked him again.

A weak smile came to Chico's lips. 'No. No-one. It's my secret place where I can be close to the animals.'

'Good. We'll have to leave you here for a couple of days but we will be back and I promise you, we will help you out of this situation, Chico.'

She squeezed his hand.

'Thank you,' he said, as he squeezed her hand in return.

They left Chico lying on his bed of ragged curtains. Indigo looked back to say goodbye but he had already fallen asleep. The three weary rescuers made their way out of the house. A sombre mood had overtaken them as they picked their way through the grounds. It was Brandon who noticed them first. Three men emerging through the hole they had made in the fence, one looking very smart in a linen suit, the other two, raggy looking.

'We're in for it now,' he said, 'here come the owners.'

'They don't look like the kind of people that would own a place like this. Wouldn't they be coming through the front gates?'

'They aren't the owners,' Indigo cried. 'It's Carlos and his men and they've got guns in their hands.'

All three stood still, as if a motion spell had been cast upon them preventing them from moving.

'Run!' shouted Letitia, breaking the spell.

She spun round and sprinted, cheetah like, back towards the house, followed a few metres behind by Indigo and Brandon. As he launched himself through the gap in the window, Brandon took a quick look back. The men were gaining on them.

'Hurry up,' he shouted, pushing Indigo through the broken window.

They made their way straight to the linen cupboard. As they burst through the door, Chico stirred.

'Chico, Carlos is here. We have to get you out of here.'

Indigo and Letitia pulled him to his feet and ran out of the room dragging Chico with them. From the top of the stairs they could hear the men struggling to get through the narrow gap in the window. They would have to find an alternative way out. They ran to the end of the corridor where they found another set of stairs leading to the upper floor.

'This way,' Chico told them.

He led them to a door and into a high ceilinged room. The walls were panelled with dark wood and an ornately carved fireplace dominated the room. They closed the door behind them, hoping that Carlos and his men wouldn't follow.

'I know this house very well,' Chico began, somewhat breathless from the exertion, 'there is secret room behind here.'

He pushed against a thin strip of carved wood framing the oak panelling. They heard a soft click and the panel opened inwards.

'In here. Quick.'

The panel closed behind them. They were in darkness. Gradually, as their eyes adjusted with the help of a shaft of grey light coming from a small grate in the wall, they could make out a dusty, wooden table in the corner of the room, accompanied by two ancient, spindly-looking chairs. Apart from that, the room was bare. Indigo sensed a mild panic rising in her. The room was small, airless, windowless and claustrophobic. She liked to be able to see the sky.

'This is just like a priest's hole in the old houses in England,' Brandon commented sitting down on one of the chairs.

'Yeah, whatever,' replied Letitia, wafting her hand in the air. 'So what we gonna do now? We in a bad situation or hadn't you realised?' She thrust her hand on her hip, her charm bracelet making its familiar harsh, jangling sound. 'We can't just wait here 'til those thugs find us. They're bound to find us.'

'Not necessarily,' Brandon pointed out. 'We have the advantage of knowing this room exists. They don't.'

'That's true,' said Indigo, trying to be positive.

'They won't leave till they find us'' Letitia added.

'She's right. Is my fault. I got you into this,' he said, speaking in broken English.

'Stop there,' Indigo raised her hand. 'We chose to help you. It was our decision.'

Letitia paced up and down the room like a depressed zoo animal.

'Speak for yourself, girl.'

'We didn't make you come here,' challenged Brandon. 'If I remember you were the one dragging us out of the hotel.'

They glared at each other. Then Indigo spoke.

'The last thing we need right now is to fall out. We need to take some time out and try to think our way out of this situation. We need to work together.'

She sat down on the floor in the corner of the room and closing her eyes took some deep breaths. It was important to remain calm she told herself.

'Hey, don't go taking all the air in here. There ain't lots to start with.'

Indigo opened one eye in time to see Letitia smiling at her.

'Just joking.'

Letitia sat down at the table. Brandon sat on the floor and took out his phone. Since the last incident at Georgina's house he had set the welcome tone to silent. He wasn't going to be caught out like that again.

'I thought so. No signal in here.'

No one spoke for several minutes. Chico lay on the floor, his eyes closed; Indigo sat with eyes closed; Brandon fiddled with his phone and Letitia picked at her finger nails. The room seemed to be filled with unspoken thoughts and unacknowledged fears until the muffled sounds of voices from the other side of the panel caught everyone's attention. Indigo put her finger to her lips and mouthed the command to be quiet. Everyone held their breath and concentrated on trying to hear what the voices were saying. The voices grew louder as they neared the secret panel sounding angry and impatient. It was impossible to make out what was being said, only the tone. Eventually, the voices faded, indicating that they had moved on in their search.

Brandon wiped his forehead and ran his fingers through his hair. 'Phew! That was close.'

Letitia pressed her ear to the panel and listened.

'They've gone.'

'You sure?'

'Pretty sure,' she shrugged.

They sat down on the floor and tried to work out how they could get out of the secret room unnoticed. The small room had begun to get airless and sticky hot.

Letitia began again.

'We can't just stay here and wait for them to find us. This is driving me mad being cooped up in here. We gonna have to do something?'

She looked across at Indigo for an answer and when it didn't come she resumed her pacing.

'How did they know where to find us?' Brandon asked. 'I thought you said no one knew about this place?'

They all turned to Chico who was still lying on the floor. He sat up, looking like a trapped animal.

'I don't tell no-one 'bout this place,' he said, defending himself from the accusing eyes.

Indigo intervened once more. 'It doesn't matter how they found us. The fact is they're here and we have to deal with that problem right now. Chico, do you know any other way out of this house?'

Chico shrugged.

'I only know the way we came.'

'That's okay. Those men will be looking in the opposite direction for us. They're hardly likely to double back. Brandon, do you agree?'

'Very possible.'

'Maybe,' said Letitia.

'Then we need to move now before they start to retrace their steps. Does everyone agree that we leave this room and find our way out of here?' she looked across at Letitia for an answer.

'Beats being stuck in here like caged rats.'

'Chico, do you think you can make it?'

'Don't worry about me. I feel better now.'

'You lead the way. We'll follow you. Nobody speak.'

Chico opened the panel and stuck his head out of the gap. A strong smell of burning filled their nostrils as they emerged from the room. Letitia looked terrified.

'They've set the building on fire,' she coughed, 'I won't be able to breathe.'

Swirls of smoke curled into the room from the gap under the door. It spread across the floor like a creeping mist. Chico opened the door letting in a wave of thick white smoke. With nowhere else to go they ventured into the corridor where the acrid smoke stung their eyes. Letitia panicked and turned to run back into the secret room. Indigo grabbed hold of her arm and swung her round to face her.

'You can do this Letitia. Remember, you are fit and well.'

'Quiet,' hissed Brandon.

They crept along the corridor to the staircase, following Chico. Once on the lower floor they made their way back to the grand staircase. They felt the heat before they saw the flames. Thick black smoke was billowing from a pile of burning ceiling whilst orange flames snaked along one side of the staircase. Flakes of burning wood floated up towards the wooden balustrade at frightening speed. It was only a matter of time before the flames took hold of the entire staircase and with it their only way out. It was obvious the route they intended to take was no longer available to them. Indigo turned to Chico. He motioned them to follow him past the staircase and along another corridor that led to the other side of the building. This time he led them down to a half landing.

'This way, through this door. I think we may be able to get out this way.'

Chico turned the handle. It turned but would not open. He stood back to let Brandon try. Brandon pushed against the door.

'It's not locked but there's something heavy behind it.'

'Let's try it together,' Letitia suggested. 'If we all push, maybe we can move whatever's there.'

They tried again, all of them putting their shoulder to the door and pushing. The door made a scraping noise against whatever was on the other side but it was no use they couldn't budge it. Letitia kicked the door out of frustration.

'They've barricaded us in. They gonna burn us alive,' she shouted, her voice breaking at the end with anger and frustration. They turned to look back. The smoke swirls were creeping along the floor towards them and licking the sides of the corridor.

Brandon slumped hard against the door. He seemed to be giving up. 'We're trapped.'

'We can't be trapped...' Indigo looked around her. 'Chico, there must be another way?'

Chico shrugged. 'Only back the way we came in.'

Back down the burning staircase, she thought, afraid to say it out loud. But she knew, looking at everyone else's expression that they were thinking exactly the same thing. Indigo took off towards the smoke.

'Come on,' she shouted, her voice full of panic, 'it's our only hope.'

The flames had spread across the staircase, making it impossible to use them to reach the downstairs window. Indigo knew they would have to act immediately. She could hardly breathe and her eyes were stinging so much from the smoke she could barely open them. Brandon appeared at her side. He was scanning the staircase to find a way down and out through the window and into the fresh air. An architectural ledge ran all the way around the reception hall, connecting with the windows.

'If we climb over the balustrade and onto this ledge, it looks wide enough for us to edge our way towards that window over there and then we could lower ourselves down the curtains. What do you think? Do you think we can make it?'

'It's worth a try. I don't think we have too many options.'

Chico stepped forward. 'I go first. I not afraid.'

He clambered over the side of the balustrade like a monkey and was soon edging his way along the narrow ledge. No-one spoke. Indigo gave up a silent plea to the universe to save them all.

No-one moved. Chico's thin little body seemed to move along the ledge like a snake. It looked effortless. He reached the window and took hold of the thick brocade curtains and swung himself free of the ledge. A sharp intake of breath from the bystanders could be heard over the crackling fire wood. It was as though they were watching a high trapeze act at the circus. Only they were part of the act this time.

Chico swung from one clutch of material to the next, managing to wind his way down to the floor below. He fell the last few feet and landed on his side but got to his feet and signalled to them that he was all right. Indigo wanted to cheer but the back of her throat felt dry.

'You go next,' she told Letitia.

Letitia looked relieved. She didn't argue. Climbing with more care than Chico she climbed over the balustrade and crept along the ledge. She looked down at one point and lost her balance.

'Don't look down,' Brandon shouted.

Letitia pressed her head to the back of the wall and continued on, looking straight ahead of her. She reached the window and stopped. Brandon shouted encouragement at her.

'Go on, you can do it,'

Letitia raised her left arm and took hold of the curtain launching herself off the ledge. She managed to grab hold of the curtain with her other hand. Success. She lowered herself down to Chico who was waiting for her at the bottom.

'You go next,' Indigo told Brandon.

'No way. I'm going last.'
'But…'
'No 'buts'. You're going before me.'
'Let's go together. Hold my hand.'
Indigo held out her hand to Brandon. He took it without speaking. With hands held tight, they edged along the ledge.

'Don't look down, you'll lose your balance,' he told her.

Indigo couldn't speak, she couldn't even acknowledge him. Her full concentration was on negotiating the ledge and reaching the floor in one piece. As they reached the curtains, a crashing sound shook the room. The burning staircase had collapsed, sending flames and burning flakes of dust swirling through the air. It startled Indigo so much she slipped and lost her footing. She screamed.

Brandon still had hold of her hand but he knew he wouldn't be able to hold on for long. There was only one thing he could do. With one Herculean effort, he swung Indigo towards the curtain.

'Grab hold,' he shouted.

Indigo saw the whole thing in slow motion. Her feet losing contact with the ledge, the sense of her body falling, then being swept up as if on a rip tide, the curtain looming towards her. She saw the loose threads of the brocade entwine her fingers and then everything from that point on went very fast.

She slammed into the glass behind the curtain, cracking it and sending shards clattering to the tiled floor. The sudden in-flow of air sent a gush of flames outwards from the balustrade, setting the curtain she was holding alight. She lowered herself down the heavy brocade until she reached the flames then pushed with her legs against the glass again and threw herself to the ground landing badly on her right leg. Despite the pain her immediate thought was Brandon.

Where is he? What's happened to him?

She picked herself up and attempted to stand. Her right leg gave way and a searing pain shot up her leg. Stumbling, she looked around for Brandon. She saw him gripping the brocade, unable to lower himself down as the curtains were well alight.

'Jump!' screamed Indigo.

'I'm too high to jump.'

Hobbling on one leg, she shouted to the others to tear down the other curtains so that Brandon could land on something softer than the tiled floor. They rushed around tugging at heavy brocades, bringing them to the floor with a thud. Through the noise of crackling fire, she heard Brandon shout.

'I'm not sure I can hold on any longer.'

'Hang on, we'll be there in a minute,' she shouted back to reassure him.

Letitia and Indigo grabbed one of the curtains together. Nothing happened. Indigo needed to do something. Somewhere from deep within her she summoned enormous strength, so much so, it surprised even her. A mighty tug at the curtain and the whole thing came toppling down on top of her. With Letitia's help, they carried the heavy curtains to where Brandon was hanging, the flames now licking at his trainers and piled them high below him. He was losing his grip.

'Jump. Now!'

Brandon kicked away from the window and dropped. Thud. He landed hard on the marble floor, twisting his foot as he did so.

'Ow,' he howled, 'get these shoes off my feet, they're burning up.'

Indigo unlaced one trainer whilst Letitia undid the other one. Once loosened, they wrenched his shoes from him and threw them away. Brandon's face twisted with pain.

'Are you all right?' Indigo asked him.

'My leg. I think it's broken.'

'Come on, Letitia; help me get him to his feet.'

The two girls struggled to lift him. She could see Brandon was in severe pain but this was no time to be gentle with him. They had to get out of there fast before they all cooked. In her concern for Brandon, Indigo had forgotten about Chico. She realised she hadn't seen him. She looked around the hall but he was not there.

They started toward the window, Brandon hopping on one foot, supported by the girls.

'Where is Chico? We can't leave him behind.'

'I haven't seen him. He was right by me a minute ago,' Letitia said, her voice catching on the choking smoke.

They reached the window and soon realised it would be virtually impossible for them to lift Brandon up and help him through. The heat was unbearable. Indigo could feel it burning her cheeks. She was beyond pain by now, her foot badly injured and her eyes streaming so much she could hardly see. They stood in silence feeling the immense hopelessness of their situation. Then they heard a commotion behind them. It was Chico running towards them holding a cage.

'My pet rat. I no leave him behind,' he grinned. 'Come on,' he said, losing no time, 'I help you with your friend.'

He placed the cage on the floor, whispering something in Portuguese to his pet before tearing off the remaining boards, creating a bigger hole to get through. Together they managed to lift Brandon up to the window and push him out the other side. Indigo winced as she heard him crash to the floor and then scream in agony.

With great haste, the two girls clambered over and dropped to the ground. Chico handed his pet rat to Indigo before hauling himself through the window, dropping to the floor like a circus tumbler.

Once outside, Indigo slumped against the wall, exhausted. Her relief at being safe was all too much for her. Tears fell down her cheeks, stinging her scorched face. She coughed as the fresh air filled her lungs. The feeling of tension release was short lived. As she sat doubled over regaining her senses a voice spoke out. She had never heard the voice before but it sent a deep sense of dread into her heart.

'Get over here, Chico,' it said.

It was Carlos. He stood, gun in hand, next to Juan and Domingo who were also pointing their guns at the exhausted party. Carlos was sneering at Chico a half smile twisting his face.

'Did you think I would let you burn in there when you have something of mine? Come on. We have some unfinished business.'

He kept his gun trained on the small figure of Chico whose eyes were wide and staring. With his other hand he motioned him to approach. Chico looked around him looking for a way to escape.

'There is no place to go. You make one move to run away and I swear I will shoot you. I don't need you alive to get back what I need.'

Indigo had never seen a gun before and she stared at it in disbelief. She hoped it might be a toy gun but she knew it was wishful thinking on her part.

How cruel to have come this far only for Chico to be caught like the poor rat in his cage. His situation is hopeless. If Chico tells him he no longer has the drugs inside him, Carlos will kill him. Will he kill us too?

It seemed absurd at such a time to start chanting a mantra but in the past it had helped her overcome stressful situations. The hypnotic effect helped to quell the sickness that was rising in her stomach.

All will be well. All will be well.

Chico appeared to be frozen to the spot. Indigo knew he must be thinking the same as everyone else. That he was in big trouble whatever he did. Carlos became impatient and lunged, full tilt, into one of his rages.

'Domingo. Bring the boy over here. The rest of you, stay where you are.'

Domingo rushed over to Chico. He grabbed hold of Chico and picked him up like he was a bag of crisps.

'Leave him alone,' shouted Letitia.

Domingo lashed out at her but Letitia was quick and dodged his blow.

Indigo couldn't think of a single thing she could do to help. She screwed her eyes shut and continued her mantra.

All will be well. All will be well.

It was difficult to say how many minutes had passed when it happened but an echoey voice jolted her from her hypnotic state. It was the sound of someone's voice through a loudhailer. They were speaking in Portuguese. Indigo didn't understand a word but she watched as Domingo released his grip on the boy whilst Carlos and Juan tried to make a run for it. A line of armed police, dressed in riot gear, prevented them from escaping.

'Drop your gun and stand away from the boy.'

The voice echoed across the unkempt gardens creating an unworldly, unreal atmosphere. Indigo felt dazed as if she were in a dream. Through a hazy fog, the police rounded up Carlos and his men, disarmed them and secured their hands behind their backs, before marching them away. She drifted away into blackness.

'Are you all right?' a voice said in broken English.

She opened her eyes to see a Brazilian policeman staring at her. He was dressed in full uniform, his gun still in its holster.

'Yes,' she answered but the words seemed not to be coming from her mouth but from somewhere in the distance.

'She's in shock. Get the doctor over here quick.'

The voice sounded concerned but faraway. She didn't remember much after that.

CHAPTER THIRTY FIVE

Indigo woke up in her hotel room with Juliet standing over her. Juliet took hold of her hand.

'How are you feeling?'

Indigo tried to sit up but slumped back down on the pillow.

'The doctor gave you something for the shock. You probably feel a bit woozy. How's the leg?'

Indigo moved her leg which she now noticed had a bandage on the ankle. It hurt when she moved it.

'Feels fine. Where are the others?'

'No need to worry. Letitia is in her own room, she has smoke damage to her lungs but she'll be fine.'

'And Brandon?'

'Brandon has a broken leg I'm afraid. But he's okay. They've fixed him up and he's going to be fine. He's just down the hall.'

'And Chico?'

Juliet sat down on the bed.

'Your friend Chico has been arrested. The police said he was wanted in connection with drug smuggling. I think you have a lot of explaining to do but that can wait.'

'The last I remember someone was pointing a gun at him,' she answered, her voice sounding far away.

'Don't concern yourself about that now. I'm sure when we get all the facts we'll be able to sort this mess out.'

'Am I in a lot of trouble?'

Juliet screwed up her nose. 'Let's just say you won't be earning any Brownie points.'

'Does mum know?'

'Yes. She wanted to fly out here straight away but I managed to reassure her you were okay.'

'Oh no! She'll worry about me.'

'I had to let her know, Indigo.'

'What's going to happen now?'

'You've all had a very lucky escape. You might not have made it. Now get some sleep.'

Juliet squeezed her hand and left. Indigo drifted back to sleep.

The next morning she woke at first light. Easing herself out of bed, she tested her foot on the floor to see if she could stand on it. It felt weak but she found she could put some weight on it without it hurting too much. She limped down the corridor towards Letitia's room. She tapped on the door and opened it a notch. Letitia lay in her bed but at the sound of her door she raised her head.

'Indigo! You okay?'

'I feel fine now. What happened? Did I faint? I can't remember anything.'

'Your eyes started rolling around in your head and, yeah, you just passed out.'

'Juliet says you've got smoke damage. How are you feeling?'

Letitia took a deep breath making her cough.

'Pretty good this morning,' she said.

'Really?' Indigo said in disbelief. 'Have you seen Brandon yet?'

'No. Let's go see him now?'

Letitia leapt out of bed and threw on a cotton dressing gown and some pink fluffy slippers.

'Let's go.'

Brandon's room was further down the corridor with the other boys in the party. They knocked and waited.

'Come in,' they heard him say.

Brandon was already up, dressed and sitting at a table, writing. His right leg was in a plaster cast.

'Does it hurt?' Indigo asked him.

'It did at the time, but it feels fine now. Just a nuisance to get around with those things.'

He pointed to a pair of metal crutches by his bed.

'Do you know they've arrested Chico?' Indigo said.

'Yes. Juliet told me last night.'

'What are we going to do?' Indigo responded.

'Now, wait a minute,' Letitia cut in, 'isn't this how it all started before? I'm not going to go through all that again and I'm certainly not breaking someone out of a South American jail. No way.' Her arms were waving about in the air, bangles jangling, and she was pacing up and down the room. 'You must be mad. Absolute crazies. You ain't getting me nowhere near no South American jail.'

Indigo looked at Brandon.

'She's off on one again,' he said, laughing.

Letitia heard them and stopped in her tracks. 'You laughin' at me, again?' she asked, her hands on her hips in that challenging stance.

She looked across at both of them and laughed. With them this time.

'What I want to know,' began Indigo, changing the subject, 'is how they found us? Do either of you know?'

Brandon explained. 'Apparently, we were spotted coming out of the hospital and followed to the house. Simple as that.'

'I suppose we haven't done enough SAS training,' Letitia said, dropping back into her sarcasm.

'But what about the police? How did they know where to find us?'

'They weren't looking for us. The police had been following Carlos for some time, gaining evidence against him so that they could arrest him. They'd followed him to the safe house thinking he was about to carry out a drugs deal, only to find Chico and three English kids. What a shock that must have been!'

Indigo laughed as the vision of how they must have looked when the police arrived flashed across her mind. The others saw the funny side and laughed with her. The laughter was curtailed by a knock at the door and a woman's voice. It was Juliet.

'Yeah, come in,' shouted Brandon.

The door opened and in walked Juliet and Kash. Kash gave them all a big, white smile but Juliet looked worried.

'I'm glad we've caught you all together. I've been talking to Kash about what we should do.'

Indigo and Letitia sat down on the bed. This sounded serious.

'He's got a lot more experience than me at dealing with ...' she hesitated, 'young people. To be honest my expertise is with animals and, after yesterday's events, I think I'll stick with animals. They're less complicated.'

She turned towards Kash, hoping he would step in and help her out.

Kash appeared to have a permanent smile upon his face. 'Yeah. Well pretty exciting stuff from what the police told us yesterday.'

He was speaking in a serious tone but Indigo couldn't help feeling that he probably didn't take anything in life that seriously. She watched him as he spoke. His teeth shone and his eyes glinted. His hands were huge, with long, well-manicured fingers which he flourished in front of him as he spoke. She could imagine him playing piano with a band for some reason.

'Me and Juliet...' he corrected himself, 'Juliet and I...have had quite a long talk about what happened yesterday and the impact this has had on the project...'

Oh no. We're going to get sent home without being able to re-home the monkeys.

'We've decided that...' he looked across at Juliet.

Indigo's heart was beating faster than a wind-up toy.

Please don't send me home.

'Well, it wouldn't be fair to the others if we didn't all go to the rainforest together,' he grinned. 'Listen,' he continued, 'this doesn't mean we don't think what you did was wrong. We both think you should have told us what you were doing and where you were going but the fact is, this whole project, from my point of view, is about character building and self-reliance. And well, I saw a lot of that yesterday.'

He looked around the room, which had fallen silent.

'One more thing...we have decided to bring our trip forward so we're setting off this morning to the rainforest. Is that okay with you?'

Indigo thought about Chico. She couldn't just walk away from him now and leave him to end up in jail.

'Can I ask you something?' she asked Kash in a quiet voice.

He nodded.

'What's going to happen to our friend Chico?'

'Well, we've also been thinking about him and wondering how you know a boy like that.'

Letitia jumped in. 'Well… we don't reeally know him. We found him on the street and we got to know him from there.'

Phew! Good thinking Letitia.

'We kinda guessed he was a street child.'

'It wasn't really his fault. The drug thing. He was forced into it. That man Carlos threatened to kill his mum,' blurted Indigo.

Kash held up his hand to silence her. 'I think I may be able to help your friend.'

'How? What can you do? Can you get him out of jail?' Indigo was speed-quizzing again.

'I have some contacts with some people out here from a charity who help street kids.'

Indigo was by now, sitting on the edge of the bed, hanging on to every word Kash was saying. Her heart was still beating fast but from excitement now, not dread.

'They do a lot of good work in Rio with street children. They may be able to help him. I can call someone and see what can be done before we set off.' Kash held up his mobile phone. 'Do you want me to ring now?'

Indigo couldn't help herself. She ran towards Kash and gave him a huge hug around his waist, burying her head into his chest. Letitia joined them.

'That makes a change,' he said, laughing, 'I'm used to getting verbal abuse from Letitia not hugs.'

'Hey,' shouted Letitia in protest.

'Come on,' Juliet prompted, 'get your things together. We need to get going. Brandon, how do you feel about this journey with your leg? Are you going to be okay?'

'Try stopping me,' he replied, jumping up from his chair and hopping on one leg to his crutches.

'We'll help him,' offered Letitia.

Kash gave Letitia a look of surprise. He hadn't seen this side of her character before and he was liking it.

'Let's get this show on the road. See you downstairs in the lobby. I'll go gather the troops and start loading up the mini bus. Great stuff Letitia.'

Kash went over to her and gave her a high five. Letitia beamed.

'I thought you said you were going to ring the charity about Chico?' Indigo asked. 'I can't leave without knowing he's going to be okay.'

'Oh yeah, I'll do it now.'

He took out his mobile phone and dialled. Indigo moved closer to hear the conversation. Realising her intent, Kash switched his phone onto speaker mode.

'Hi. Is Rowena there?'

'Who shall I say is calling?'

'Tell her it's Kash from England.'

'One moment, please.'

The phone went silent. Kash made a face at Indigo. She smiled back at him and then a voice came on the line.

'Kash? Hey, hi there. Are you phoning from England?'

'No. I'm in Rio?'

'Rio! And you haven't come to see me?' the voice reproached.

'Sorry Rowena. I've been busy.'

'Too busy to come and see me?'

There was a slight pause then Kash carried on. 'I have a huge favour to ask you?'

'Yes, go on, what is it?'

Kash explained what had happened to Chico and that he was in custody at the local police station. He asked her if there was anything she could do to get him out of jail.

'I think I may be able to help,' she said. 'We have a lawyer we can use who has a good relationship with the local police. If he can get this boy Chico released into our custody they're usually okay with that. They know we'll look after the boy and help him. I'll get onto it right away.'

'That's fantastic, Rowena. I knew you'd be able to help.'

'No worries. So when am I going to see you?'

'Not sure. I'm off to the rainforest north of Recife any minute now. Maybe when I get back?'

She laughed. 'I'll hold you to that.'

'I owe you one,' Kash replied and ended the conversation.

'Happy with that?' he asked Indigo.

'I guess so,' she replied. 'You will you let me know what happens to Chico?'

''Course I will,' he said, giving Indigo one of his big smiles.

CHAPTER THIRTY SIX

It wasn't long before they were bumping along a dirt track on their way to their destination deep in the heart of the rainforest. The monkeys were being transported by special carrier and would meet up with the group the next day when they arrived at camp.

Indigo spent most of the journey drifting in and out of sleep. Letitia talked most of the way, re-telling the events of the previous day to her friends. Indigo could see why she was a natural leader. She had a way of talking that made people listen even if her language wasn't always the Queen's English. She listened to the many questions being asked about how and why and noticed that Letitia was very careful not to mention anything about Indigo's unusual involvement. She smiled to herself, grateful for Letitia's protection. The air conditioning hummed in between bursts of reggae coming through the speakers from Kash's iPod.

Occasionally, he would sing a chorus of a well-known Bob Marley song and everyone would join in. The atmosphere was relaxed and joyful. Indigo felt calmer now knowing that something would be done to help Chico. Kash had made contact with the charity and they had promised to help. She turned her thoughts to Mango.

What would her reaction be when she saw the rainforest again?

Since her visit to the monkey sanctuary and the chat she had with Juliet about caged animals she had done a lot of thinking. A change of heart about keeping her pets. She loved them all and although she realised releasing them into the wild now would mean certain death, she had decided not to add to her collection. In future, she would spend her pocket money on wildlife conservation projects – not on caged pets.

The journey took several hours and by the time they reached camp which was a tented activity centre somewhere deep in the rainforest, they were all pretty exhausted. A Brazilian man, called Guito greeted them. He showed everyone to their tents and pointed out the meagre facilities. A toilet block which was no more than a hole in the ground, a kitchen which was a circular pile of rocks on which a spit had been rigged and the wash room which was a fast running, rocky stream.

'This is just like 'Get Me Outa Here, I'm a Celebrity,' Letitia announced.

'Yeah, get me outa here now,' her friend grumbled, kicking at the ground.

Indigo could sense the city group were not impressed by the camp. She, on the other hand, found it magical. The early evening light filtered through in a filigree pattern, growing darker by the second. They were surrounded by lush vegetation and a thick canopy of trees. Indigo noticed the smell was entirely different to that of the English countryside, more like an earthy, mossy smell with notes of perfumed blossoms. She lost herself in the sounds of the rainforest. Unlike the city children she felt a deep connection to the land.

Animal sounds in the distance, rustling through bushes, exotic bird sounds and fast running water crashing over rocks. She couldn't wait for Mango to arrive and watch her first tentative steps out of her transportation cage and back onto the cool, brown soil of her home.

Guito set the fire going and they spent the night sat around the camp fire eating sausages and telling stories. He knew so much about the area and the people living in this part of the rainforest. He brought everything to life. Indigo sat quietly, listening to him. The effects of the tranquilliser and the long journey were beginning to take effect. Her lids felt heavy and she nodded once or twice, waking herself up. When he mentioned he was going to visit a village the next day, Indigo couldn't help herself. Despite her tiredness, she dived in with a plea to be allowed to go with him. Guito looked across at Juliet and she nodded.

'Can Brandon come along?'

Guito shook his head. 'I'm sorry, young man. You would never make it with your leg.'

Brandon shrugged, accepting the fact that his leg would be a problem.

Indigo turned to him and whispered, 'You don't mind if I go, do you?'

'Heck no,' he said, looking down at the ground and picking up stones to throw into the fire.

Juliet looked across and nodded at Kash. They both stood up.

'Time for bed, guys,' Kash announced. 'Big day ahead for all of us. Let's get some kip.'

Indigo slept well that night unlike Letitia who was struggling with the lack of toilet facilities. She was still getting ready for bed, taking off her makeup and whatever else she was fussing over.

'Ain't there no mirrors in this place?'

She was still muttering to herself as Indigo drifted off to a restful sleep, perfectly at home in her current surroundings.

Kash had organised several outbound activities for the next day so he and Letitia's group disappeared quite early to climb rock faces. Indigo could hear them complaining about the heat, their aching bones and the fact they had to carry their own heavy rucksacks. She felt sorry for Kash but he seemed used to that behaviour. She heard him singing Bob

Marley as they trooped into the rainforest and disappeared from view.

Indigo couldn't wait to get going. After they had eaten breakfast, she said her goodbyes to the others and set off with Guito in his Jeep to visit the nearby village. Guito had some business with the village elders. Indigo wanted to know how people survived out in the rainforest and why so much of it was being destroyed. Guito explained that until only recently in this part of the rainforest people had lived off the land hunting and foraging but that was beginning to change. Large areas of the forest had been destroyed to make way for crop growing such as soya beans or cattle grazing for McDonalds. This was destroying the delicate balance of the rainforest's eco-system and would have long term, unknown effects on the whole of the planet.

Indigo listened as they drove along paths lined with the charred remains of trees and undergrowth. They passed a huge area of blackened earth. Her mood had changed to one of sadness. She could see before her the destruction of this beautiful and special place. In the distance she could see a group of men hacking down tall trees. Lorries were coming and going carrying away long, straight logs which Guito said would be sold and made into mahogany furniture. Once the tree was felled, the rest of the forest was burnt to blackened earth. A sadness like no other she had experienced before overwhelmed her, as she looked at the scene of devastation before her.

This can't be happening. How could man be so cruel to Mother Earth?

Guito carried on, stopping at a small clearing.

'We walk from here,' he announced, turning off the engine and jumping from the jeep.

Indigo followed him as he made his way through dense undergrowth to a clearing. They had arrived at the village. Guito approached a group of old men who were sitting under the shade of a huge tree. He spoke to an old man who held out his withered hand to shake his. A small group of children were playing together in the clearing. She caught the eye of a small boy. A look of recognition passed between them. It was Itamar. She walked over to the children, leaving Guito to talk business with the men.

'Itamar, it is you, isn't it?' she asked, not quite believing it was really him.

'Indigo, what you doing here?' he spoke broken English in a heavy accent but she could understand him.

'Guito brought me. I've brought the monkey with me.'

Itamar looked confused.

'You know the two monkeys we talked about?'

He nodded.

'I rescued them. The mother died but the baby survived.'

His face lit up at the news and he broke into a broad grin.

'What's happening here? Why are they cutting down the trees and destroying this magical place?'

Itamar shrugged, then hung his head, remaining silent.

'What's the matter?' she asked him.

'The elders, they make the decisions. We had no choice.'

With an understanding and wisdom way beyond her years, she understood his problem and those of the villagers. They were just trying to survive in any way they could.

'I understand,' she said, placing her hand on his shoulder to re-assure him.

'I could not stop them but now they want to become farmers. It is better than stealing the animals? No?'

'But that is destroying the rainforest and when the rainforest is destroyed where will the animals go? They will have nowhere. We are killing the earth. Can't you see?'

'No this is different.'

Guito approached just then.

'Ah, I see you have met Itamar. He is a good boy and will be useful to us in our project here. He is a quick learner.'

'Project?'

It was Indigo's turn to be confused now.

'Yes, we have exciting plans for this village. I will tell you on the way back. We must go now or you will miss the release of the monkeys.'

'I'll keep in touch,' she whispered to Itamar.

She was leaving the village with a stirring of hope in her heart. On the way back, Guito explained the new project that he was working on with an organisation called the Rainforest Alliance. It sounded very exciting.

'Did you notice the tree the elders were sitting under?'

'It looked like the Mimosa tree in my mother's garden,' Indigo replied remembering the tree.

'Well spotted. It is a member of the Mimosa family. We call it an Angico tree. There are a lot of those trees in this region and the government has given them a high conservation status. The Alliance is carrying out research into the medicinal properties of the tree. If they can harvest it, economically, the villagers can make a living without destroying vast areas of the rainforest.'

'That sounds fantastic. Will it work?'

'I think there is a good chance. The research has shown that the bark and gum is good at treating asthma and all sorts of other conditions. I am very hopeful.'

'Oh, I really hope so because this is such a special place. It breaks my heart to see it being destroyed like this.'

'You have a good heart,' Guito told her.

Back at the camp, the monkeys had arrived. Indigo ran over to Mango's cage to check on how she was. Mango looked back at her with sad, brown eyes almost human like and stretched out her arm through the grille. She gripped Indigo's hand.

It's going to be all right. You are home. You are truly home.

'We've been waiting for you,' Juliet shouted over.

Mango jumped away at the sound of Juliet's voice and darted around inside her small cage. Indigo whispered more words of comfort before the cage was lifted up and carried away by the helpers. Indigo walked with Brandon who was making slow progress on his crutches. With great care, they laid the cage on the ground and opened the front, standing back out of sight. At first only her head could be seen peeking out from inside the cage. Then she climbed on top and looked around. It looked as though she didn't want to leave. Indigo closed her eyes.

Go on. Your family is here. Go and find them. It's time to go.

Mango looked in turn at Indigo, then Juliet, then behind her towards the dense undergrowth. She leapt off the metal cage and ambled on all fours towards the bushes. Just before she reached them, she turned again. She seemed to be hesitating.

Go on. That way.

Mango looked at her with sad eyes.

They're waiting for you.

Mango nodded her head and scampered into the bushes, disappearing from sight for ever. Indigo saw that Juliet had tears in her eyes.

'She'll be okay,' Indigo told her.

She took out a tissue and wiped her eyes. 'I know. I always get emotional at this point. I can't help it.'

They returned the empty cage to the truck. As they were packing up they heard the familiar sounds of a barrel of monkeys close by. It sounded to Indigo like a celebration cry.

The return of a lost loved one.

CHAPTER THIRTY SEVEN

'Mum!' screamed Indigo, rushing through the arrivals lounge and throwing her arms around Demelza.

They hugged each other for a long time and when Indigo finally let her mother go, she noticed tears on her cheeks.

'I'm okay, mum, really I am. I've had such a fantastic time.'

Demelza wiped the tears from her eyes with a tissue.

'I know, darling. I'm just so pleased to see you.'

Indigo kept tight hold of her mother's hand. Luke was there waiting for Brandon. Their greeting was less emotional.

'Brandon. How you feeling?'

'Great,' he said from his wheelchair, lifting his leg up to expose a plaster cast on his right leg. 'I'll be better when I get this off.'

'I thought he'd get his first broken leg playing sport, not escaping drug barons,' Luke joked, tousling his son's hair.

Indigo had insisted that Letitia meet her mum before leaving and had dragged her over.

'Mum, this is my friend Letitia.'

Letitia held out her hand to greet Demelza.

How old fashioned. Not like Letitia!

'She's from London and we've promised to keep in touch. Haven't we?'

Letitia said 'hi' to Demelza and Luke before turning to Indigo to give her a big hug.

'I'd better go. Kash is waiting to take us home. I'll text,' she shouted after her.

Indigo watched as her friend made her way through the crowds.

'Bye,' she shouted but Letitia didn't hear.

A sense of loss washed over her at the thought of losing touch with her new friend. She turned to her mother.

'Mum, can we invite Letitia to stay with us soon?'

'Course you can, sweetheart, although I'm not sure what she'll make of the sleepy old Cotswolds?'

'More to the point,' Brandon cut in, 'what will the Cotswolds think of her?'

They all burst out laughing as they picked up luggage and made their way to the car park.

'I've got so much to tell you mum. It's been awesome.'

Luke drove them back from the airport. Indigo and her mum sat in the back. Throughout the entire journey Indigo and Brandon competed with each other to tell their parents all about their trip to Brazil.

When they arrived at Indigo's house, Demelza invited Luke in for a drink but he declined saying he wanted to get Brandon home. They said goodbye and Demelza thanked Luke for the lift. Indigo noticed her mother gave him a kiss on the cheek.

That's a new development.

She dumped her suitcase in the hallway and ran straight upstairs to check on her pets. They were all there, just as she had left them. She collapsed on the bed, hugging her favourite animal, Leopardy, a tiger she had bought from a trip to the Rainforest Cafe.

'Home. So, so good to be home,' she told Leopardy.

Her thoughts turned to Chico. She hoped he was somewhere safe. Just then, she noticed a letter propped against her alarm clock on the bedside table. The stamp looked foreign. On closer inspection, she could see it had come all the way from Brazil. She sat up and grabbed the letter, tore it open and pulled out the hand written pages.

'*Dear Indigo,*'

It began…

'*Someone from the charity has kindly offered to help me write this letter.*'

It was from Chico.

'*The charity has helped me get a job in the zoo here in Rio working with the animals. Now I won't have to steal to buy a ticket! But the best thing in the whole world is that they found my mother for me and we are now living together in a small apartment. My*

Indigo read and re-read the letter several times. Kash and Rowena had promised to help him and they had kept their promise. Chico's life would be different now. He was safe and he was happy and he was with his mother. Tears filled her eyes until the writing on the paper became blurred. She was crying from a mixture of sadness and great happiness. Happiness because Chico had been re-united with his mother and he would no longer be forced to lead a dangerous life and sadness for all the children who were not as fortunate as her.

She lay there feeling a tremendous sense of gratitude for her lovely home and her lovely mother. She realized just how lucky she was to have both. She placed the letter back in the envelope and put it on the table. Hugging Leopardy, she sunk her head into the soft pillow and stared out of her skylight. She turned over in her mind all the things that had happened in the last few weeks and wondered how she would adjust to ordinary life? School loomed ahead. The summer holidays were nearly over and she would be back doing lessons, not driving through rainforests. A tingling sensation prickled the back of her neck. She knew that feeling. There would be more

adventure in her life. She just knew it. Only just
what kind of adventure she couldn't be sure.
The 'knowing' was enough for now.

247

Printed in Great Britain
by Amazon.co.uk, Ltd.,
Marston Gate.